Praise for *T.*

"Tish Thawer's intriguing story line is weaved and crafted into a magical and spellbinding web that kept me up until the wee hours of the morning biting my finger nails and cheering for the sisters. Strong story line and well developed characters that will sweep you away. I was completely floored by this amazing book and I recommend it to everyone.!" ~ *Voluptuous Book Diva*

"Tish Thawer is an amazing wordsmith. I have devoured several books by her and she never disappoints. The blend of history with contemporary is just genius and I can't wait to see what this author will come up with next. Add this to your list as a must read recommendation from me! An EASY 5 out of 5 stars!." ~ *NerdGirl Melanie*

"Overall, The Witches of BlackBrook was a grand slam for me. I was so enchanted by this spellbinding tale of hope, love, and a bond that can't be broken. There was something special about it and I honestly think it had something for all different types of readers. Whether you're into romance, historical, paranormal, new adult, etc. the author effortlessly weaves so many elements together to create a flawless experience for whoever picks it up. If you're looking to be enchanted and escape your mind for a couple hours, I highly suggest picking up The Witches of BlackBrook and diving on in!!" ~ *Candy of Prisoners of Print*

Praise for *Scent of a White Rose*

"Thawer managed what I thought was an impossible feat. She was able to put yet another new spin on the age old vampire tale." ~ The Bookshelf Sophisticate

"...everything about *Scent of a White Rose* was such a fresh new concept when it came to vampires, actually it was just a whole new concept in general for the paranormal genre! This is a read any paranormal lover should read!" ~ YA-Aholic

"*Scent of a White Rose* is not the plain Jane girl meets vampire and falls in love story...I will tell you that you should add this book to your TBR list." ~ The Book Nympho

"Tish Thawer crafts a seductive vampire tale with her eloquent writing style and keen sense of romance that simply entrances." ~ Romancing the Darkside

Praise for *Aradia Awakens*

"Tish Thawer is one of those authors whose works are marked by something incredibly special. With each book she writes, I am awed by the magickal elements in each novel." ~ Author Rae Hachton

"The author skillfully weaves a tale so intense that you can't help but want more." ~ The Cover and Everything in Between

"Once more, I was overwhelmed by the creativity and imagination that comes from this author..." ~ Proserpine Craving Books

"I really, really like the world of Ovialell. The world is unique, complex, and full of all sorts of paranormal species. There are werewolves, vampires, amazons, Goddesses, there are so many interesting elements to the world." ~ The Book Savvy Babe

Raven's BREATH

THE WOMEN OF PURGATORY BOOK 1

by

Tish Thawer

Amber Leaf Publishing
Divide, CO

First Edition
First Printing, 2014
ISBN: 978-0615995786
Library of Congress Control Number: 2014905722

Front cover design by Regina Wamba of Mae I Design and Photography
Full-wrap design by Emma Michaels
Edited by Nancy Glasgow

Amber Leaf Publishing, Divide, Colorado
www.amberleafpublishing.com
www.tishthawer.com

Acknowledgements

To my wonderful family—I couldn't dream what I dream without you. I love you guys with all my heart.

To Cortney and Des—Your input means more to me than you know. Thank you both for listening to me rant and rave. Without those times, magic couldn't happen.

To my amazing cover artist and friend, Regina Wamba—Thank you for inspiring this story with your amazing talent.

To Emma Michaels—Thank you for enhancing my vision and bringing Raven to life.

To my editor Nancy Glasgow—Thank you for your keen eye and constant professionalism.

Death's firm grip settled on my arm. When I spun around, the serious look on his face caused my internal alarms to sound.

"Raven, when was the last time you were sent to Heaven during a retrieval?" His voice was strained and taut.

I pulled from his grasp and took a quick step back, contemplating the odd question. It wasn't unusual for me to visit Heaven, or Hell for that matter; it was part of my job.

"Earlier today, why?"

His jaw clenched, then he and Holli disappeared. Wow. Guess I won't be getting an answer.

I shook my head and took to the sky, finally heading home for the night. As I neared my apartment, I saw Garrett rushing up to the main door of my building. I adjusted my trajectory and touched down gently behind him.

"Hey! Fancy meeting you here."

"Actually, it's not fancy at all." His intensity shook me. "I need to talk to you."

"What's wrong?"

"Let's get inside." He ushered me into the building and up the stairs to my apartment with the urgency of an undercover spy on a mission.

I flipped the lock. He unceremoniously pushed me inside, slammed the door, spun me around, and pressed my back against it.

"What are you doing?" I demanded.

"I need to check for something." He brushed the hair away from my ears then turned my head from side to side. This is awkward. "Garrett, seriously, what the hell is this about?"

"Not Hell."

"What?"

"Hold still." The edge of panic in his voice had my heart racing. He continued to run his thumb over the smooth skin behind my ears and down each side of my neck. "Oh my God, he was right," Garrett breathed.

I'd had enough. I shoved him off with enough force to push him away from me. "What are you talking about?"

"You've been marked, Raven."

I stared at Garrett like he was an idiot, but it was I who was completely clueless. "Marked? By what? What do you mean?"

"I mean..." He grabbed my arm and pulled me to the mirror hanging next to the front door.

"...Heaven has marked you."

1

Sirens blared, cutting through the still night, while I watched from the shadows. A man who'd just been hit by a taxi lay bleeding on the frigid, grime covered ground. People began to gather and were staring at the gruesome scene, while the driver of the taxi sat on the curb, crying into his hands.

I scanned the crowd, singling out who'd seen death before and who hadn't.

I could always tell.

My attention snapped back to the dying man when he took his last breath. Images began to take shape in his mind; images that due to my *job*, I, too, could see.

Snapshots of him riding a motorcycle for the first time, of him falling in love, of his big successful promotion at work...all images of him. It was the usual replay of one's life flashing before his eyes.

When the replay stopped, it was time for me to go to work.

I stepped out of the shadows and took two steps in his direction. To the people watching, his wide eyes marked his final passing, but to me they continued to grow as he took in my features: dark hair blowing in the wind, a curvaceous body wrapped in tight black leather, and large wings the color of the night sky. No one could see me but him, for he now resided in the netherworld...in my world.

I extended my hand and offered my usual greeting. "My name is Raven, and I'm here to help you find peace." He reached for me, then glanced back to take a final look at his body.

"Am I really dead?"

"Yes."

"And you are..."

"The Grim Reaper."

This was the exact conversation I'd had with thousands of souls, which was why I knew that *now* would be the best time to comfort him, before he got scared to death—no pun intended——and tried to flee from me.

I extended my wings and let my divine light radiate from within. "There's nothing to fear."

This usually worked since I looked more like an angel with wings than the old man with a scythe that most people envisioned. Maybe that's why I'd been chosen to become the first female Reaper in history; the boys had been losing too many souls.

My inner light built to its crescendo, opening the portal to Heaven. It was through a Reaper's inner light that all souls were transported to their destined eternity, whether it be Heaven or Hell.

I guided the man to the pearly gates, then quickly returned the same way to the earthly plane and flew to the highest point of the Holy Cross Cemetery. It was the oldest and largest in the "city of cemeteries," Colma, California, located just south of San Francisco. I tucked my wings into my back and walked up the hill, the heels of my boots sinking into the dirt that surrounded the large mausoleum.

The name over the ornate stone entrance read Richard Payman, Born 1892 - Died 1962. I placed my hand on the door's handle and the letters R. and P. became illuminated. I smiled when the numbers shifted and transformed into the sum of their total—1+8+9+2+1+9+6+2, equaling 38. In other words...Reaper Portal, Thirty-eight.

There were thousands of portals, each one located in a cemetery tomb that read Richard Payman, Born "something" – Died "something else," to indicate which location you were entering.

The seam of the door glowed blue, then opened to reveal the shimmering orb waiting within. If a human opened this door, however, all they would see was a stone sarcophagus holding *Mr. Payman's* remains.

The portals were the only entrance to our world; the world of Death and his Reapers, a.k.a. Purgatory.

I stepped through and the city greeted me. A wide expanse of dark stone buildings and gothic turrets dotted the light gray sky. Inky tendrils swirled and floated through the air, extending as far as the eye could see.

The black smoke-like wisps were the souls that refused to move on—the phenoms.

Whenever a soul tried to flee, they would instead "stick" to the Reapers until we returned to Purgatory, where they were sucked into the sky to wander aimlessly for all eternity.

Poor bastards.

I flew towards the main building, hoping to check-in and be done before I started my long weekend. I touched down on the slate steps and took a moment to compose myself before entering the massive castle.

At present, I was the only female Reaper in Death's employ, but according to rumors, I wasn't sure how long that would be the case. It didn't surprise me; I'd been a huge help in lowering the numbers of lost souls, but to be honest, I wasn't sure if I wanted to share the title of "*one and only.*"

"Good evening, Raven." My eyes shifted. Death's long bony fingers wrapped a staccato beat against the round heads that made up the armrests of his creepy skull throne. "How are you?"

All Reapers worked for Death, but I doubted anyone in Purgatory actually liked being in his presence. Then again...maybe it was just me.

"I'm great, thank you. I was just checking-in before I headed home."

A smile played on his lips. "While I always enjoy seeing you, you shouldn't feel obligated to check-in with me. Your numbers are consistent and you haven't let me down yet."

His words carried an edge that left me worried I'd somehow done exactly that. I swallowed hard against the lump in my throat, nodded and turned away.

"Raven, a quick question before you leave?" Death asked, polite as always.

A slow breath escaped my lips. *So much for a speedy escape.* I turned around slowly and plastered a smile on my face.

"Sure. What's up?"

"I've been thinking about bringing on another female Reaper—since you've proven to be such a valuable asset," he added. His leer made my skin crawl. "But I wanted to talk to you first, of course, before I made my final decision and see what you thought of the idea."

Ha! Like he gave a damn what I thought. He'd do whatever he wanted, and I knew without a doubt this was just his way of watching me squirm.

I tossed my hair over my shoulder and smiled. "Actually, I think that's a great idea. I've been playing clean up for so long, it might be nice to have a little help around here."

Hmph. I don't squirm.

2

I headed straight for Garrett's, my footfalls echoing loudly on the cobblestone street. He was my best friend, and if you needed information, he was the person you went to. As Death's accountant, he was always in the know.

The activity in his apartment was frenzied. Reapers rushed in and out, updating him with their totals. I was up to one-hundred and twenty-seven so far this month. *Not too bad!*

"Hey, Raven, you look a little singed. Did you have to take another trip to Hell today?" Garrett's voice carried over the low rumble in the room.

When I'd first become a Reaper I'd imagined having Garrett's job would've been great—sitting behind a desk, working from home, knowing all Death's juicy little secrets. But

7

after witnessing how hard it was to keep up with the business-end of people dying, I quickly became *very* satisfied with my field assignment.

"Nope. Just got back from saying 'Hey' to St. Peter. How about you? Rough day?"

"Nah...just busy as usual. I'm getting ready to shut down, though, if you want to wait. We can go get a drink once I open the night drop."

"Sounds good. I actually start my vacation tonight so I'm totally ready to get this party started!" I said, gyrating my hips in an awkward motion.

Garrett's chest vibrated with a hearty laugh. He knew I wasn't a drinker and my idea of a vacation basically involved me sitting around my apartment, watching old movies, and taking dips out the window to fly amongst the souls. Yeah...I was kind of a hermit, so the idea of me "partying" was a pretty big joke.

Garrett finished scratching pen to paper then led the remaining Reapers from his apartment and threw the lock. With a swipe of his hand a horizontal mail slot appeared in the middle of his front door. People didn't stop dying just because it was the end of our day. Reapers worked twenty-four hours a day, seven days a week, three-hundred and sixty-five days a year. But Garrett was only one man and apparently the *only* man Death trusted with his assets. When Garrett wasn't working, we simply tossed our totals through the night drop. I'd often wondered if he got tired of waking up to a shit-ton of paperwork scattered in his entry every single morning, but he never complained.

"So, have you heard anything else about Death wanting to bring on another female Reaper?"

I couldn't hold my tongue any longer. Garrett had been the one who'd told me the rumor in the first place. At the time I'd been too shocked to actually consider it, but now, with Death throwing it in my face, I figured it was time I dug a little deeper.

"Nope. Just the initial peek I caught through his gazing pool of a woman with white wings."

"Hmm. So you haven't actually seen any paperwork about a new Reaper, just the image of a female in Death's *magic puddle*?" I couldn't help the skepticism or the sarcasm in my voice.

"Well, yeah. You're the only Reaper with wings, Raven. Wings that he gave you when he recruited you. I assumed he was doing the same thing with her."

"That makes sense, I guess." I stuck my hands in my pockets and continued to walk towards the bar as the memories of my rebirth flooded my mind.

In my human life I'd been an RN; a single nurse completely focused on my career. My parents had passed when I was in my teens, and I didn't have any siblings. At the age of twenty-two, I'd died alone from a disorder called TIAs— Transient Ischemic Attacks.

It was something I'd suffered with for most of my life, the episodes usually passing after a few minutes. This particular time, however, it didn't pass; it killed me.

A blood clot had moved through a small vein in my brain, causing stroke like symptoms. When I realized this attack was different from any other I'd experienced before, I'd struggled to reach the phone. My hand was inches short of the receiver when my body collapsed on the living room floor. Once my spirit rose out of my body I was greeted by a Reaper—Daniels if I remember correctly—but just as I'd reached for his hand, another appeared and shooed him away.

I had stood face-to-face with Death himself, and he wasn't at all what I expected. Tall and thin...yes, almost skeletal to a point, and creepy as hell. But it was the black designer suit and midnight blue tie that completely threw me, not to mention the utter politeness and charm he displayed. The contradiction between the myth and the man was glaringly obvious.

I stood there, completely stunned, as he offered me a job. He explained it was a once in a lifetime opportunity and if I were to accept, he'd give me special "perks" that no other Reaper had—wings.

I'd collapsed back onto the couch, dumfounded and still in shock over my sudden departure from the human world. I couldn't fathom the afterlife I was being offered, but couldn't deny that the idea of continuing on as someone so special was indeed a heady thought.

My life had been filled with mild successes but nothing I'd consider remarkable. I'd never stood out in any way. But suddenly, in the moment of my death, I'd been given an opportunity to become something extraordinary. The chance to further my career or better myself in any way had ended the second my heart had stopped. But as a Reaper, I'd be able to help those who'd lost their life's battle and be the one to guide them to their final peace. The allure of that was overwhelming, and simply something I couldn't pass up. However, I didn't accept his offer right away. Instead, I'd spent what seemed like hours drilling Death about the details of his organization and what the job would entail. He'd explained my duties, all while trying to convince me that it would be great, that I would have my own apartment and all the earthly things I could ever want.

I couldn't have cared less about those things, but considering the alternative, I finally agreed...on one condition. He had to give me my wings right then and there—before I went anywhere with him—to prove he was for real. I was flabbergasted when he actually did.

One moment, I was my normal human self—albeit in spirit form, and in the next, Death materialized a raven out of thin air and melded the creature to my back. I was instantly transformed from Raven—the twenty-something nurse who'd just died, into Raven—the first female Reaper in history with black wings and the power of Death flowing through her. I took my new employer's hand and disappeared, emerging back in his chamber. Death showed me to my new apartment and introduced me to Garrett, who had me sign some papers before winking at me as I'd left his office.

The following day Death hosted a grand party where he announced my arrival.

It was chaos.

An entire world of male Reapers pulsed with anticipation of having a female within their midst, but when Death declared I was to remain un-touched—at the risk of their final deaths— the excitement quickly turned to disdain. I'd instantly become the one thing they all wanted but could never have.

It took me about week to find my way around Purgatory, but only a couple days to realize I'd be better off if I stayed secluded in my room. I'd always been somewhat of a recluse so the adjustment was an easy one to make.

I'd started retrieving souls within my second week and as my numbers climbed, Garrett and I had become fast friends. Other than the ever-present tension in the air, everything

Death had told me seemed to be on the up-and-up; that had been almost twenty-five years ago.

"Does it really bother you that there could be another female Reaper? Maybe the two of you will end up being really great friends." Garrett's question yanked me from my memories. I turned to him, ready with my smartass reply before I caught the smirk plastered across his face.

"Why, yes, you never know. Maybe we'll be BFFs and paint each other's nails, and talk about our boy problems while sitting around in our sexy pjs."

By the time we got to the bar we were both shaking from laughing so hard. The idea of me being best friends with anyone other than him was utterly ridiculous. Garrett accepted me and always knew just how to take my mind off of work and the stress that came with it. That was just one of the many reasons why I loved him so much. I was smiling wide when we entered the club arm-in-arm, ready to relax.

Then I saw Krev.

3

While I may not be a people person, I still managed to come to terms with the male population and got along with almost everyone...except Krev. He was such an asshole, and for some reason he seemed to carry a real chip on his shoulder when it came to me, one that to this day I still couldn't understand.

"Well, well. If it isn't the infamous, Raven." His mocking tone and the shitty look on his face confirmed he was trying to start a fight, as usual.

"Hey, Krev. Bad day? Let me guess, you lost some more souls? Oh wait, that's not a bad day for you...just a normal one."

The small crowd around us snickered in the background.

"Actually, Raven, I didn't have anyone run from me today, but there was this one lady who refused to go until she made sure someone found her body. It was awkward. She was chatty. I learned how to cross-stitch while we waited."

His humorous response caught me off guard. Usually nothing other than pure hatred flowed past his lips. I took the opportunity to remove myself from the confrontation.

"Well, at least she didn't run from you. Looks like you had a good day after all." I started to turn away when he asked another question.

"Why, did you have a runner?" His eyes widened at the excitement of my potential failure.

I took a deep breath. *Just walk away, just walk away.* I knew I shouldn't engage him, but I couldn't help myself. With his usual dickhead behavior etched into my brain, I cocked a hip at his ridiculous question and flared my wings. "Now come on, Krev. You know better than that. No one runs from me."

Krev threw his hands in the air. "Oh, that's right...beautiful, Raven, the best Reaper in the business. You've got it easy, tight ass, nice tits, and an awesome wingspan. You wouldn't do so good if you didn't have those wings and were stuck wearing this shit." He lifted the edge of his cloak and released it with a disgusted flare.

"You're right. I suppose if you guys had wings and weren't required to wear those drab things you'd be doing a lot better in your numbers and I wouldn't have to constantly clean up your messes," I jibed.

Shortly after I was recruited, a bunch of phenoms found a way to break loose from their Reapers in New Orleans. In order to stop them from overrunning the city as ghosts, Death sent me on the first ever gathering mission, giving me yet another perk to do the job. Reaper ribbons were smoky black tendrils that looked like the phenoms themselves, but were actually attached to me. When projected, they wrapped around the souls who'd fled, allowing me to snag and transport them back to Purgatory when no one else could. Ever since, I was the one they called to track down the runners whenever a breakout occurred.

Maybe that was why Krev had such a problem with me. Not only did I have wings when he didn't, but I'd also received a second perk from Death. I couldn't imagine his hate was born from something as petty as jealousy, but maybe I was wrong. Maybe it *was* that simple.

"Fuck you, Raven. You think you're so special, but even if Death did let you date, nobody would want you. Guess it's a good thing you like being alone!"

The fissure his words caused within me elicited a strange dueling reaction. My first thought was to rip him limb from limb, but at the same time, I wanted to spread my wings, burst free of this place, fly home, and cry my eyes out. I, of course, could do neither.

Reapers weren't allowed to fight without immediate punishment, and I would never give him the satisfaction of seeing how his digs affected me. So I stood, frozen; words of retaliation crystallizing on my tongue.

4

After Garrett read Krev the riot act, making sure to use as many expletives as he could, we continued our "relaxing" evening back at my place with a bottle of wine.

"Thanks for standing up for me back there, Gar. If I'd have opened my mouth, even for a second, I would've ended up beating the shit out of him and spent the weekend being punished for it."

"You're welcome. Krev's a douche and deserves all the crap he gets."

Garrett and I laughed and talked the rest of the night away. I threw a blanket over him once he fell asleep. His broad shoulders filled the width of my small couch and his long legs dangled off the edge.

Garrett may be a pencil pusher for all intents and purposes, but he was one of those hot geeky types that when you looked close enough, you could see he had a real Clark Kent/Superman vibe going on. He was tall and built, with dark hair and beautiful blue eyes. I loved him, in a big-brother sort of way, and times like these only solidified how lucky I was to have him in my life. I smiled wide, grateful for a pleasant end to a hectic day.

I entered my bedroom and caught sight of the phenoms floating gently outside my open window. They may be lost souls, but once they entered Purgatory, any connection to their Reaper was severed and they simply became smoke-like clouds that drifted peacefully throughout the sky.

I debated taking a brief flight amongst them, but decided against it when my eyelids drooped. Instead, I wrapped my wings around myself and crawled straight into bed.

Images of a woman filled my dreams. She was standing in front of a mirror, her back to me, primping and preening at her own reflection. I couldn't make out her face, but she was lithe, with long platinum hair, and wings as white as a new-fallen snow.

This was the new female Reaper Death was recruiting, I was sure of it. As if he'd heard my thoughts, Death appeared from the shadows and came to stand behind the woman. He placed his hands on her shoulders and whispered something in her ear. I couldn't hear his words but the slight roll of her hips made it clear they'd been sexual in nature.

My dream shifted and was replaced by a memory, one of me standing in Death's chamber declining his latest advance. Images flickered behind my eyelids. The words *'I'll never be interested in being anything other than your employee,"* tumbled from my lips. The replay was disjointed, skipping from moment to moment. I'd been as polite as possible when he'd started hitting on me after forbidding anyone else from doing so, and even managed to maintain my sickeningly sweet smile as I walked out of the room. His low chuckle, echoing behind me, had sent goose bumps racing over my skin. For me, that was the moment Death had become the bad guy history portrayed him to be.

I bolted upright, my chest heaving. I swear I could still hear his sinister laugh resonating inside my head. I grabbed my gray silk robe and padded into the bathroom. A quick splash of ice cold water on my face helped to ease the tension. I looked into the mirror and had an epiphany.

Death was lonely.

5

The carpet beneath my feet was worn thin by the time I heard the rustling of blankets and sounds of Garrett stretching. *Finally!* I threw open my door and rushed into the living room, ready to begin my interrogation.

"Has Death ever dated anyone?" I blurted out.

Garrett looked up at me with a bewildered look on his face. "What?"

"I want to know if Death has ever dated or been in love with anyone."

He shook his head and repositioned himself upright on the couch, untwisting his wrinkled plaid shirt and smoothing the legs of his jeans. "Um...not that I recall. Why?"

"I think I figured out why he wants a new *female* Reaper." I crossed my arms and wiggled my eyebrows.

Garrett's laugh was boisterous and I suddenly felt less like Sherlock Holmes and more like Inspector Clouseau from the Pink Panther.

"I'm serious! For years after I was recruited he would always hit on me, and last night I had a dream that this new female was going to be filling a very specific *position* for him, if you know what I mean."

Garrett pushed off the couch and headed for the kitchen, pouring us both a cup of coffee. "I don't know, Raven. Maybe. But you just said it was a dream, so I highly doubt the woman you saw was actually 'the one.'"

"Well, she had platinum hair, a white satin dress, and white wings, so I'm pretty sure it was her. Besides, my dreams have been more than just dreams lately, you know that."

For the past few months, ever so often, one of my dreams would end up being a presentiment. I'd catch a glimpse of someone and later that day, during a retrieval, I'd end up face-to-face with that same person. I'd contemplated asking Death if it was another perk he'd bestowed upon me, but since it had happened only a few times I'd decided not to bother.

"Okay, fine. But if it is her, so what? She can be Death's girlfriend and you can continue to do your job with no reason to feel threatened. Unless of course you're rethinking Death's propositions?"

Coffee spewed from my lips. "Are you insane? I would never, and I mean NEVER, date Death. EVER."

Garrett laughed. "Now you sound like that Taylor Swift girl."

By the time we finished cracking ourselves up and eating our sausage links, French toast, and scrambled eggs, I was feeling lighter and excited to start my vacation. It had been so long since I'd had more than a single night off, I'd painstakingly scheduled my three-day weekend to include as many activities as I could.

First on the list was a stop at Drey's Boutique. Drey was a wiz on the sewing machine, and I was in need of some new clothes.

"You hanging with me all day, or do you have stuff to do?" I asked Garrett.

"I would love to, but I have to head to work for a meeting with the big guy. I can catch up with you after that, though, if you'd like."

"Okay. Buzz me when you're done and I'll let you know where I'm at."

"Sounds good." Garrett kissed my cheek and saw himself out.

I finished cleaning our dishes then took a quick shower. Dressing in minutes, my ripped jeans, gray suede boots, and soft v-neck T-shirt were a welcome change from my usual leathers.

All my clothes had to be custom made, due to my wings, hence my visit to Drey's.

I walked through the shop door, smiling when the little bell announced my presence.

"Raven! How are you, beautiful?"

Drey was one of the few Reapers Death used for business purposes instead of field work. Just like Garrett, he had a nine-to-five job. He was a tall black man with a bald head and a heart of gold.

"Hi, Drey. I'm good, thank you. Just looking for some new leathers."

"Fantastic. Flip that lock and let's get started, girl."

I did as he asked and stripped down to my bra and underwear. I'd never been self-conscious about my body, but especially not in front of Drey, seeing I wasn't his "type."

"How's business?"

"Not bad, considering the only thing I have to do is provide you with custom shirts, Death with designer suits, and supply all these gorgeous Reapers with a replacement cloak every now and then."

I laughed, shifting slightly on my feet. I doubted any of the jobs here in Purgatory were actually enjoyable when you considered the monotony.

After an extravagant wave of his hand, Drey got right down to business. He re-measured me, though in death my size would never change. I'm sure the habit was just that...a *habit* from his previous life as a tailor.

I stood stock still while he draped me in swaths of new material, the buttery leather cool and soft against my skin.

In no more than thirty-five minutes I was redressed with a bag of shirts and a time to pick up my new designs in a few days.

"Thanks again, Drey," I said, zipping up my boots.

"You're..."

A knock on the door drew our attention.

"Raven, could you get that, please?" Drey called from behind the counter.

"Sure."

The man behind the glass was holding a large flat box. I smiled and unlocked the door. He handed me the parcel and held out a slip of paper to be signed. Drey crossed the room and reached for the slip but not before I caught a glimpse of another signature already on it.

It was Garrett's.

My curiosity shot through the roof. I waved goodbye to the man and turned back to Drey. "Oohh, what's in the box?"

"Actually, I'm not sure."

6

He lifted the lid and my stomach dropped.

It was a pure white satin dress—the same dress the woman in my dream had been wearing, and apparently Garrett had ordered it. "Who is that for?" I couldn't hold my tongue.

"Again, I'm not sure. But according to the note inside, I'm suppose to put it in back and someone will be by later today to pick it up." He shrugged like the mysterious package was no big deal.

My head threatened to burst and my wings ached. I was losing control. I had to get out of here before my inner light ignited, and I sent Drey on a ride straight to Heaven or Hell.

"Is something wrong, Raven? You look like you're about to go off."

"I'm sorry, Drey. Thanks for everything, but I have to go."

I rushed from the shop, extended my wings, and shot into the air. Flying always helped to calm my nerves, and right now I definitely needed to calm down, or I was going to kill Garrett. How could he lie to me? Apparently, he *had* known more about the female if he'd ordered her a fucking dress. *UUUGGHHH!*

I pushed faster into the gloomy sky, closing my eyes and letting myself drift amongst the phenoms, their soft wisps caressing me as I flew. Rain pelted my face, and I began to relax, the drops washing away the sting of betrayal I couldn't help but feel. It was one thing for Death to bring on a new female for whatever purpose, but it was another for my best friend to lie to me about it. I thought it was the bite of the storm against my skin that reminded me that while I was technically dead, I was still very much alive, but in reality, it was the pain piercing my heart that drove the fact home.

I soared through my window and threw the now soaked bag of shirts onto the bed, following them down until my face was buried in my periwinkle duvet.

Jolted by the buzzing in my pocket, I dug out my phone and snarled as I read the text. *"GARRETT: Just got done with my meeting, where you at?"*

I debated texting back, *"In Hell, wanna come meet me!"* but I doubted my angry response would have made much sense to him at the moment. So, instead I simply replied, *"At home."*

"Cool. Wanna grab lunch in an hour?" How could he act like nothing had happened? Like lying to me was an everyday occurrence? *Hmph.* Maybe it was.

"Where?"

"Digger's?"

"See you there."

Could he sense the anger in my snappy texts? Did he have any idea the fury he was about to face?

Highly doubtful.

Forty-five minutes later, the inside of my cheek was raw. I couldn't wait any longer. I darted back out of my bedroom window and veered towards *Digger's.* It was one of Garrett's and my favorite restaurants. The atmosphere was that of a graveyard, with eerie lighting, tombstones, and caskets intermingled throughout. Top that off by the fact that the owner, Digger, had been an actual grave digger in his previous life, it was all rather poetic.

I pushed through the heavy door and walked to the furthest booth in the back. It was a semi-circle of black leather and brass studs, the curved back reaching high above my head. *Perfect.* While I didn't think our conversation was going to be a pleasant one, I wouldn't embarrass Garrett or myself in public.

"Hey, Raven!" Garrett excitedly slid in next to me.

"Hey." I lowered my head, avoiding his eyes. Apparently my subdued response wasn't enough of a giveaway to my mood, because Garrett immediately started rambling on about his meeting.

"Raven! Are you even listening to me?"

I wasn't. Clearly. But the second I started paying attention my anger fizzled like a cheap ball of bath salts.

"I just told you that I know the identity of the new female Reaper, and you're not going to believe this! Death had me special order a dress for her this morning. A white satin dress, just like the one you saw in your dream!"

"Wow. That is crazy."

"Oh, and her name is Holli...with an 'i'," Garrett stated.

Of course it is.

Garrett and I continued to discuss what he'd learned during his meeting. Apparently, Death had given him the same old story about wanting another female Reaper to help collect the lost souls.

I shook my head. I wasn't buying it. I couldn't forget the sexual tension that overshadowed what I saw in that dream.

"I'm telling you. There's more to it than that," I argued.

"Well, I'm telling you, that's all I know. Her name is Holli, she'll be here tomorrow night, and he demanded that a white satin dress be sent down from topside immediately."

"Tomorrow night, huh? I wonder if he's going to keep her all to himself for a while, or make a big presentation of her?"

"Actually, there's a party scheduled for All Hallows Eve."

"Oh for fuck's sake. Can he be any more dramatic?" I wanted to gag at the fanfare I knew Death would be putting on.

Garrett laughed at my obvious disgust. "Come on, Raven. It's only a few days away, and you know how he loves the holidays. It's only natural."

"Are you defending him?"

He shrugged. "Defending him against what? He hasn't done anything wrong. He's recruiting another female Reaper and will be announcing her at his favorite party. So what! If you remember correctly, we celebrated you for at least a week straight when you showed up."

I flopped back against the booth, crossed my arms, and tried to reel in my bottom lip. He was right. It was Death's choice to bring on whoever he wanted for whatever reason, and presenting them to the rest of Reapers at a party had always been a normal occurrence. So, why was this bothering me so much?

Jealousy, plain and simple. Whether Holli was meant to be Death's girlfriend or not, she was still a hit to my ego.

"Raven, just let it go. You will always be the *first* female Reaper in history, no matter how many other women Death drags into Purgatory."

I reached for his hand and smiled. Again, he was right. *Now, if only I can get rid of this terrible feeling.* I had ice in my veins.

7

Garrett and I spent the rest of the afternoon finishing my errands which included a trip to the dry cleaners, a run to the market, and a visit to a liquor store called *The Last Stop*. It was now early evening on the first day of my vacation, and I had no idea what to do. Normally, being alone was my first choice, and I was comfortable with that, but I couldn't deny the needling feeling that I should be living it up before Holli arrived and completely shifted my world.

Live it up? *Ha!* We lived in Purgatory for crying out loud. An endless expanse of gray and gloom, reminiscent of old London. I supposed Garrett and I could run across the rooftops, pretending one of the phenoms was the infamous Mr. Hyde, and see how we'd fair at tracking and catching the notorious beast, but instead, I simply took Garrett out for a flight above the rooftops. When we returned, I found myself happier and more at ease than I thought was possible only a few hours ago.

"That was fun! I don't remember the last time you took me flying." Garrett flopped down on my couch, out of breath.

"Yeah, it was, we should do it more often. Hey, do you want some wine?"

"Sure. That sounds good."

I popped the cork, poured two glasses, and returned to the living room. Garrett was just about to reach for his when a loud knock resounded from the front door.

I looked at the clock and glanced at Garrett. His eyebrows lifted as he shrugged his shoulders.

"Who is it?" I called out.

"Death."

I froze, the glasses threatening to slip from my grasp if I took even one more step.

Death had never visited my home before, and his appearance here tonight did not bode well.

"Just a moment, please." I didn't know what else to say. I sat my glass down and took a second to gather my thoughts. I didn't want to seem flustered in front of Death, in fact, I always made it a point not to.

I opened the door. "Please come in." With a swipe of my hand I gestured inside.

"Thank you, Raven. I'm sorry to call on you at this hour." The ring of sincerity in his words surprised me.

"Of course, it's fine. Garrett and I were just sitting down to watch a movie. How can I help you this evening, Sir."

Death stole a quick glance at Garrett before continuing. "Unfortunately, I have to cut your vacation short. Another outbreak of phenoms has just been reported topside. I'll need you to start gathering them right away."

My shoulders fell, and I exhaled sharply.

"Is that a problem?"Death asked, his terse tone enough to snap me to attention.

"No. Of course not. Just let me get changed, and I'll be on my way."

"Great. You'll need to use portal seventy-five."

I started towards my bedroom but halted when Death continued.

"Oh, and Raven, just one more thing."

8

I turned around and froze. Standing in my living room was the beautiful Holli, her white wings filling my doorway as her satin dress pooled on my floor.

"Raven, this is Holli. I'd like her to accompany you tonight."

I clenched my fists. Was he kidding? I couldn't believe this. Not only had Holli showed up a day early, but now he thought it was a good idea to shove her down my throat on a mission?

"Um, with all due respect, Sir. I don't think sending a new recruit on a gathering mission as their first assignment is a good idea. As you said yourself, I need to hurry, and she would only slow me down." I lifted my chin and crossed my arms.

The look on Death's face sent chills down my spine. Silence hung in the air and Garrett seized the opportunity to jump up from the couch and reach for Holli's hand.

"Hi, Holli. I'm Garrett. It's nice to meet you."

I'm gonna kill him. How dare my best friend speak to her, let alone be nice to her.

"Hello." Her voice was sweet and soft, just as you'd expect. *Gag.*

I stared, taking in her porcelain skin, dark gothic makeup, and long platinum hair. I wanted to rant and rave, to verbalize all the venomous thoughts pooling on my tongue, but with Death's icy stare boring into me, I quickly gained control of my emotions and introduced myself instead.

"I'm sorry. Where are my manners? Holli, I'm Raven and it's very nice to meet you. Please understand, I meant no disrespect, but gathering missions are a bit...*different* from our usual retrievals. I wouldn't want you to become overwhelmed on your first assignment."

I wasn't sure if Death was buying my concern, but Holli seemed to be.

"Thank you. I'm so nervous to get started, but definitely excited to learn from the best."

Awesome. A suck up.

I met Death's gaze and knew I didn't have a choice.

"All right. Let me change and we'll head out." I nodded at Death and asked, "Have you given her Reaper ribbons as well?"

"No, but Holli has perks that should come in just as handy."

Cryptic...Great!

"Fine. Give me five."

I stomped into my bedroom, slammed the door, and ripped a pair of leathers off a hanger in the closet. Five minutes later, I was dressed and standing in front of the mirror, my dark hair and black wings a complete contradiction to the snow-white angel waiting in my living room. I shook my head and walked out to rejoin the crowd and caught Holli removing her hand from Death's forearm. The gesture was small but spoke volumes.

"You ready?"

"I think so," she smiled tentatively.

I glanced at Garrett, who was still plastered at the end of my couch. "Lock up for me?" I asked.

"Sure. No problem."

After escorting Death from my apartment he turned and added, "Raven, you should know that until I've officially introduced Holli to the other Reapers, she will remained cloaked—shrouded by my magic. No one but you, Garrett, and me can actually see or communicate with her."

With no further explanation he smiled at Holli, wished us luck, and disappeared, leaving me and the *invisible girl* to make our way to the portal fields.

In Purgatory the portals were housed in mausoleums, exactly as they were topside, but here they were laid out in rows of tens, covering an area of about two square miles. Death had said to use portal seventy-five, so after walking to the seventh row, we strolled down five spaces to the mausoleum we were looking for. I yanked open the door and gestured for Holli to enter.

She hesitated. "Where will we end up?"

"I don't know."

"What should I do when we get there?"

"Stay out of my way."

Already sick of the exchange, I pushed passed her and entered the glowing orb. A split second later I was overlooking Tokyo.

Holli emerged and would have slammed into my back if I hadn't moved. "This way," I commanded.

I could see the phenoms circling a building in the distance. There were at least twenty, which was damn odd, seeing as most outbreaks only numbered in the single digits.

"Have you used your wings yet?" I asked.

"Yes. I've been trained."

I glared at her. How could she have possibly been trained if she wasn't supposed to arrive until tomorrow night? I was about to pose my question when she interrupted my train of thought.

"It looks like the longer we wait the more ghosts appear."

Her soft voice annoyed me, but not as much as the fact that she was right. The cloud of phenoms seemed to be growing. *What the hell?* "Let's go."

I pushed into the sky and felt Holli do the same. Her form was good and she glided smoothly beside me.

The building had a flat roof which made for the perfect gathering point. I landed, tucked in my wings, and stretched out my hands.

Ribbons left my fingertips just as Holli stepped up beside me. I turned my head and it was as if the world had dropped into slow motion.

Holli stood next to me with a large silver sword raised high above her head. The weapon glowed, its metal engulfed in a purple light which highlighted the etched symbols along its blade. It pulsed, as if alive, and the swirling mass reacted.

I stood and watched the phenoms twist into a vortex and soar towards us. Holli never moved as the souls were sucked straight into her massive sword.

It was over in the blink of an eye; an entire cloud of escaped phenoms gone while Holli retracted her magical weapon.

"I call it The Devourer." She clipped the now small, charm-like knife onto the chain belt that cinched her gown and shrugged like she'd just tucked away her sunglasses.

"The Devourer?"

"Yes. It's one of the perks Death gave me. I like it."

"I can see why."

She had to speak again to snap me out of my daze.

"Do you think that's all of them, or should we make a sweep of the city?"

"Um...yeah. We probably should," I stammered.

Holli pursed her lips and tilted her head, probably in response to the *under*whelming impression I was giving so far. Who could blame her? One mission and I'd become obsolete.

I pushed off the building and flew into the cobalt sky. The stars twinkled and lit up Holli's wings, making them sparkle. She looked like an angel sent straight from Heaven.

My blood boiled, and I surged faster into the night. I may have disliked the idea of her arrival before, but now, with her gliding gracefully beside me, dislike was too mild of a word.

As we darted in and out of Tokyo's famous high-rises, I spotted three more clouds of phenoms writhing at the top of three different buildings.

"You take this one, I'll get the others," I instructed.

Holli nodded and landed on the building closest to us. I watched her raise "The Devourer" into the air once more and shook my head in disgust.

I landed on the next rooftop and immediately flung out my Reaper ribbons. They easily wrapped around the escaped souls and began to retract with the black mass fully in tow. It was the most runaways I'd ever gathered at once.

The large ball of swarming ghosts got closer and closer, and I wasn't sure how I was going to get to the next batch without dropping these off first.

That, of course, was when I heard Holli yell, "Do you want me to get the last of them?"

She hovered above me, her hair blowing in the wind and her sword poised at her side. She looked like a warrior princess.

Dammit!

"Yes. That'd be great. I'll head back to the portal with this bunch."

"Okay. I'll be right there." She took off like a shot towards the remaining cloud.

My nostrils flared. I wanted to stomp my foot through the roof of the building, freeing the angry beast inside of me who was clamoring to escape. But instead, I flew back to the portal to finish my mission.

The instant we returned to Purgatory, all the phenoms were sucked into the sky, adding their black inky souls to the dismal gray expanse. I turned to Holli. "We need to let Death know what just happened. I've never seen anything like that before. Usually I've only collected five or six runners at a time," I explained.

"Oh, he already knows. That's why he wanted me to come with you. He told me there would be a lot more souls to gather tonight."

The angry beast inside me howled, its cry filling my head.

9

I paced my living room after busting through the front door, scaring the crap out of Garrett, who'd decided to wait for me.

"Garrett, I'm telling you, something weird is going on. She said Death already knew there would be a lot more souls to gather this time. How did he know that? He's never been able to predict what we'd be facing topside before."

Garrett slumped into the couch and exhaled a long breath. "I don't know, Raven. Maybe he's figured out a way to use his gazing pool to see the future." He shrugged.

I glared at him and huffed at his lame excuse.

He threw his hands in the air and exclaimed, "Well, shit, I don't know!"

I had to think this through and if Garrett was only able to offer assumptions, he wasn't going to be much help to me. I needed to be alone.

"Well, I guess I'll sleep on it and let you know if I think of anything tomorrow." I gestured towards the front door.

"You kicking me out?"

"Yep."

"Fine, but promise you'll actually sleep and not stay up all night, freaking out about this, okay?"

"I promise."

Four hours later all I could see were the tiny red pixels of my digital clock through squinted eyes—2 a.m. Even after all the brainstorming I'd done, I couldn't come up with a logical explanation to how Death could have known about the extra phenoms. I'd contemplated Garrett's comment over and over. It was widely known Death's gazing pool was a way for him to see topside, but now, I'd begun to wonder if Garrett was right. Was Death's pool somehow becoming predictive in nature?

Exhausted, I flopped back onto my pillow and hoped to get a couple hours of sleep, keeping my promise to Garrett, if only minimally.

Tonight's dream wasn't of Holli, but instead of the runaway ghosts we'd collected and their brethren. I saw massive groups of phenoms in cities all over the world, swarming like bees around rooftops and trees. It was as if they were balloons and someone had cut them free, causing them to float up and up until they hit an invisible ceiling.

Lucid dreaming wasn't a skill I'd honed, but I made the effort to turn around and search the scene for clues. Nothing else stood out or struck me as odd, so after one last look at the cloud of souls, I told myself to wake up.

This was the hard part. Sometimes I'd get caught in-between, knowing I was dreaming and thinking I was awake only to realize I was still asleep. *Wake up!*

As my eyelids fluttered, I saw one more thing; Death stood in a candlelit room, holding a large scythe, surrounded by souls.

I rolled over and reached for the pad and pen I kept next to my bed. The dream was cliché, but regardless, I didn't want to leave out anything when I talked to Garrett about this. Maybe together we could take these pieces and complete a puzzle that would somehow make sense. If not...it looked like Holli and I were going to become very busy in the near future.

I scratched down all the details I could recall. The massive clouds of runaway souls, the names of the cities I'd recognized; New York, Seattle, and San Francisco. The shape and items in the room where Death stood. I closed my eyes and concentrated, hoping to remember at least a few more det.

Seconds ticked by, and I began to drift back into that spac, between conscious and unconscious thought.

Holy shit! My eyes snapped open, and I grabbed the pad again, quickly drawing the balloon that hovered behind Death's head.

10

I hammered on Garrett's door, regretting that I'd sent him home last night.

"Open up. I have to talk to you."

I didn't care it was only six a.m. on Sunday morning. It was imperative that I told Garrett what I'd seen.

"Garrett! Come on, man. Wake up!"

"I am awake, Raven."

I spun around to see Garrett strolling up behind me with fresh coffee and donuts in hand.

"Oh my God, I love you."

"I know."

I followed him in and grabbed a cinnamon twist and the caramel spice latté he'd bought just for me.

"I figured you'd be banging down my door this morning, so I got up early and ran out for some grub."

"You're a life saver. Did I mention that I love you?"

He laughed. "Yes, yes you did, and I love you, too. Now tell me what you got."

I sunk into his oversized chair and crossed my legs. "Okay. So I thought about what you said, and I don't think this has anything to do with Death's gazing pool, but I do think he's behind the increase in runaways."

He squinted at me over the rim of his styrofoam cup while I laid it all out for him. By the time I finished it was, well...seconds later, because I was talking a mile a minute.

"Basically, I think he's found a way to snip the souls before the Reapers have a chance to retrieve them. I just don't know why he'd do that. It goes against everything the Reapers stand for."

Reapers were bound by free will. The souls had to choose to come with us in order to move on. Even running was a choice. Only I, and apparently Holli, were exceptions to the rule since we could gather and bring them to Purgatory against their will.

The slight change in Garrett's demeanor would have gone unnoticed by anyone other than me. I scooted to the edge of my chair and leaned forward, setting my coffee down and steepling my fingers.

"You know something. What is it?"

Garrett sighed and set his cup on the table. "I can't tell you."

"Excuse me?"

"I think I might know something but I'll have to do a little digging to confirm my suspicions."

"Garrett! Tell me what you know right now!"

He pushed up off the couch and started pacing. "I can't, Raven! If I'm wrong we'll be in trouble, and if I'm right...we'll be in *big* trouble."

Oh shit. "That bad?"

"Potentially."

Damn! As curious as I was, maybe I didn't want to know after all.

"Is there anything I can do to help?" I asked. I didn't want Garrett getting into a mess just because I had another *potentially* prophetic dream.

"Nah. Let me poke around a bit and see what I can find. Just keep doing what you do, but don't let on that there's anything wrong."

Easier said than done.

I rounded out my weekend with two more gathering missions, both of which Holli accompanied me on at Death's *request.* We'd established a system that seemed to be working pretty well. I would head straight for the largest cloud of phenoms, while she would pick a centralized position between the smaller groups and suck them in all at once with her sword. She ended up with a higher number of souls, but I was almost to the point of not caring. Almost.

"Do you want me to get the last group, or can you snag them on our way back?" she asked.

Don't be prideful, don't be prideful. "No, you go ahead and grab them, I've already got a hundred or so here."

She didn't even stop as we flew by, but simply held The Devourer in the air and made a bee-line for the portal. The phenoms trailed behind her like black contrails streaking through the sky.

I exited the mausoleum and paused, taking time to watch as the phenoms were added to the thickening black atmosphere. If this kept up, the souls would choke out any remaining gray, casting Purgatory into eternal darkness.

11

The next day was All Hallows Eve, the day of Death's favorite holiday and the party where he would introduce Holli to the rest of the Reapers. I was anxious to see how they would react. I had a pretty good idea but was trying to hope for the best and prayed that Krev wouldn't scare her off with his usual meathead behavior.

I looked into the mirror and checked my reflection once more. Waves of my hair fell across my chest, cascading in all the right places, accentuating my cleavage. The black strapless gown I'd ordered from Drey arrived last night, and I was very pleased with its cut. The bodice wrapped around my torso in sort of a twisting motion which carried through to the sleek skirt. It wasn't skin tight, but hugged my curves enough to make any man's mouth water, or so I hoped. I wanted to look good if I was about to be upstaged.

A knock at my front door kicked my evening into gear. I grabbed my purse from the dresser and headed to greet Garrett.

"What the hell?" I exclaimed.

He stood there in jeans and a T-shirt, and with a five o'clock shadow.

"I thought this was a formal affair?"

"It was, before it got cancelled." Garrett pushed past me and headed straight for the kitchen where he raided my fridge, grabbing an ice cold beer. "Nice outfit by the way, you trying to give the rest of the Reapers a heart attack?"

I shook my head. "Thanks. No. Wait. What? What do you mean cancelled?"

"You heard me. Death cancelled the celebration. I just spent the last hour trying to talk him out of it, but he said he didn't want to introduce Holli to the Reapers and plans to keep her shrouded indefinitely."

I racked my brain, quickly searching for an explanation, and remembered the image of them together from my dream. I didn't think Death could fall prey to a human emotion such as jealousy, but then again, if he was lonely and Holli was the first girl he'd made his own, then yeah...I could see the green-eyed monster having its way with the master of us all.

"Do you think he's just jealous and doesn't want her around other guys or do you think it has something to do with this whole, secret...snipping the souls, thing?"

"I'm not sure, but I'm definitely going to keep digging. I've known Death for a *very* long time, and he's not acting like himself. I need to find out why."

12

Soft sunlight bathed the nursing home as the woman before me took her last breath; a woman I'd recently seen in my dreams.

Her last thoughts filtered through my mind, and her spirit lifted from her corpse.

She smiled. "I knew you'd be coming soon."

You'd think it would be easier when they were expecting you, but sometimes it only made it harder.

I smiled gently. "Are you ready?"

"Yes." She closed her eyes and reached for my hand.

My inner light reached its peak, and we arrived in Heaven seconds later.

I wasn't surprised.

I'd been visiting Heaven a lot more often than Hell lately, and I knew when I'd seen this kind woman that I'd be taking her to find peace there as well.

Her spirit was greeted by St. Peter and after another blinding light, I was back on the earthly plane, ready to return to Purgatory and meet with Garrett.

We'd both spent the rest of week doing our jobs and "acting normal," but behind the scenes he'd been spending every waking minute investigating and digging into Death's secret.

As I stepped out of the portal I noticed the thick swath of phenoms that filled the sky just above my head. My chest tightened. *I sure hope Garrett has some news.* I flared my wings and flew straight home, gliding gently through my window and rushing to change clothes.

I poured two glasses of wine and set out the pizza I'd picked up for us to nibble on while we got down to business. I'd let my mind wander throughout the week, imagining all kinds of possibilities as to the reason behind the growing number of phenoms. But regardless of all my contemplating, I still couldn't meld two ideas into one cohesive solution.

I popped a piece of pepperoni into my mouth and glanced at the clock—7p.m. Garrett was late. I knew I should sit tight and wait until he arrived, but I couldn't. My body tingled and my nerves buzzed. I walked into my bedroom, intent on diving out the window, when a knock echoed through the living room. I breathed a sigh of relief and crossed back to the door.

"It's about time. What took you so long?"

I gasped, my field of vision filled with white.

Holli.

"What are you doing here?" I asked.

"Death sent me. There's been another outbreak."

Shit! Could this girl's timing be any worse? Garrett should be here any minute, which couldn't happen a moment too soon. We had to get to the bottom of this because things were spiraling out of control.

"How about you get this one on your own?"

"Really? You believe I'm ready?"

"Yes, Holli. You've been doing great. I see no reason why you can't just go and hold up that sword of yours and do your thing."

Her giggle amused me. Did she really think I cared about her training or the success of her missions? *Whatever...*

"All right. I'll go by myself, but I'm coming straight back here to let you know how it goes," she said, her excitement bubbling to the surface.

I reached out and patted her on the shoulder. "Okey dokey."

After a flurry of ivory feathers and maybe even a hint of fairy dust, Holli was off. I rolled my eyes and headed back to my bedroom.

I dove out the window and flew straight to Garrett's. It wasn't like him to be late.

I landed outside his apartment and banged on the door.

"Garrett, are you in there?"

No response.

I knocked again...*Bang, bang, bang.*

"Garrett...are you okay?"

No response. *Dammit!*

I looked around and took a deep breath. I needed to process the scene before I went ballistic. The night drop was there in the door, which told me he'd finished his day as usual. If he hadn't gone straight to my apartment, where else would he be? I tried to remember if I'd told him that I would pick up food or not; maybe he stopped for takeout.

I took off for *Digger's* but got distracted mid-flight. There was a group of Reapers gathered around something lying on the street below me. I blinked twice and practically fell out of the sky.

It was Garrett.

13

I landed so hard the Reapers jumped, the crumbling stone under my feet a replica of what I was feeling inside. I knelt down next to Garrett and ran my hand over his forehead, trying to rouse him. "Garrett, can you hear me?"

Thankfully my torture didn't last long. His eyelids fluttered, and he started to wake.

"Raven?" he whispered.

"Yeah, Gar. I'm here. You okay?"

He sat up slowly, took a shallow breath, and propped himself up on his elbows. "Um...I think so. But how did I get here?"

I looked at the small crowd of Reapers with a questioning gaze. Each of them offered nothing more than a slight shake of their head.

"I was hoping you could tell me that. What's the last thing you remember?"

He looked around with a furrowed brow. "Um...I remember finishing up early, then opening the night drop." Suddenly, his eyes snapped to mine, awareness layering his features. "I was on my way to..."

His lids fell and his eyes rolled back in his head.

"Garrett!! Stay with me."

I scooped him into arms and shot into the sky. I landed back in my apartment in under thirty seconds. Easing him onto my bed, I felt his forehead with the back of my hand again. This time he was burning up.

I ran into the bathroom and soaked a wash cloth with cool water. Racing back to his side, I placed it on his head, sat next to him and reached for his hand. *How can this be happening?* We were already dead. We couldn't get sick, and technically, we couldn't even really hurt each other. Hence the reason Death punished us for any infighting. What was the point of beating on each other, when only he could truly hurt us.

Oh my God! That was it. Death did this to Garrett.

I pushed off the bed, intent on confronting the son-of-a-'tch, only to be halted by a knock on my door. Seething, I ᵔped across the living room and ripped it open, practically ˙ it from the wooden frame. "What?"

Holli flinched, then lowered her head. "I'm sorry. Did I disappoint you?"

"What?"

"On my mission, I assume you were watching, did I do something to disappoint you?"

What the hell was she talking about...watching?

"I have no way of watching you from here, Holli. I assume you did just fine since you're back in record time and in one piece," I snapped.

I knew I'd touched on something when a perplexed look marred her usually pristine features. "I don't understand. Death always watches me when I'm topside, and since you're my trainer, I thought you would be doing the same."

Hmmm. This seemed intriguing.

I forced myself to calm down and invited her in, hoping she'd reveal something about Death that could help me. "I'm sorry. Why don't you come in, and we can talk about it."

She smiled. "I'd like that very much."

If I was to use this little chat as an interrogation, I needed to appear present and interested. I offered Holli the food and drink that was meant for Garrett, but after watching her take a few delicate bites, my patience had already worn thin. "So exactly how does Death watch you? And is that how you were already trained before arriving here?" I asked.

"Yes and no. Now he watches all my missions through his gazing pool, but as for my training, he actually came topside to conduct my lessons. He visited me every day for months, before and after my death, to teach me how to fight and fly."

Her words nagged at me, as if this little tidbit was a *major* piece to the puzzle, and probably why Garrett was laying knocked out in my bed. *Thank you, Holli.* I couldn't wait to bring this up to him and see what he had to say on the subject. It felt important.

My excitement made it difficult to continue the conversation on an even keel, but I had to focus. "He taught you how to fly *and* fight? Why would you need to know how to fight, it's not like the souls can hurt us?"

"I'm not sure. Death only said that there may come a time when I would need to be able to protect him and myself. He demanded that I be well-rounded in my skills."

What the hell? This situation was becoming more and more convoluted by the minute. I continued to talk to Holli about her solo mission—which, as suspected, went off without a hitch, then told her "good job" and walked her to the door.

"Thank you for having faith in me, Raven, and for taking the time to speak with me. Other than Death, you are the only other person I see."

I frowned as I contemplated her words. How, and more importantly, why was he still keeping her under lock and key? I was starting to think it had more to do with her mysterious purpose here than any petty jealousies. It was obvious Death had big plans for the girl, plans that even she seemed unaware of. "Holli, have you been on any regular retrievals yet?"

"No. Death says my only job here is to help you collect the phenoms and protect him."

I couldn't stop the slight shake to my head; I just wasn't getting this. I desperately wanted to badger Holli and demand more information, but thought better of it and bid her goodbye. I quickly headed towards my bedroom, eager to check on Garrett.

My heart sank.

The bed was empty and he was gone.

14

Fuck! Had Holli tricked me? Had she been the distraction Death needed to spirit Garrett away before we could talk?

I dove out my window and flew straight to the main castle. I wanted answers, and I wouldn't stop until I got them. I couldn't comprehend why Death would hurt Garrett or steal him away from my care. Unless, of course, he'd actually found out what Death was really up to.

I didn't bother entering through the main door, instead I landed with a resounding thud on the balcony outside Death's chamber.

The room was empty, and my boots clicked loudly on the black marble tile. His throne was polished, the skulls gleaming in the candlelight that bathed the room. The ornate wall sconces and gothic furniture portrayed the macabre feel you'd expect in the chamber of Death.

I made my way across the space, vigilant and alert.

I walked past the dais on which his throne sat and entered the back part of his chamber.

Suddenly, I found myself on the edge of an oubliette, my toes teetering on the edge.

I looked into the seemingly bottomless pit, fear searing my insides, and prayed Garrett hadn't become a recent resident of the ancient prison. Once my eyes adjusted to the lack of light, however, I realized it wasn't an opening in the floor but instead a pitch black expanse of water that I instantly recognized as Death's gazing pool.

I bent down and placed a fingertip to the calm surface to verify my find. *Yep, this is it.* This was how Death was able to see topside.

I flattened my palm over the surface, running it back and forth. I was mesmerized by the ripple I'd created, so much so that I didn't hear Death creeping up behind me.

"Raven?"

Shit! I bolted upright, practically jumping out of my skin.

I realized, too late, that the room hadn't been empty after all. If Death had truly been gone, my initial entrance would've been blocked, and therefore, access to his chamber denied. *Geez. Think, Raven. Think!*

We stood, encased in silence, neither one of us willing to break it. However, the smug look on his face and the thought of Garrett in pain, quickly reignited my anger and loosened my tongue.

"What did you do to Garrett? Where is he?"

Death stared at me for a fraction of a second before answering. "I'm not sure what you're talking about, Raven. I haven't seen Garrett since yesterday afternoon."

Bullshit! I knew he was here somewhere, but I also knew Death wasn't going to just let me wander through his castle looking for my best friend.

"I know you did something to him. Why would you hurt him? Is it because he figured out the secret you're keeping?"

The instant the question left my lips, I knew it was a mistake and began to tremble.

Death visibly grew in stature. His shoulders widened and his skeletal chest inflated. The air around him grew thick, almost to the point of choking me.

I began to inch backwards, edging around the side of the pool in an attempt to escape the menace now rolling off him.

"And what would you know of my secrets?" his voice boomed.

I clenched my jaw, struggling to contain my unease. Once I made it to the opposite side of the pool, I risked a glance around the chamber. His scythe was resting in its holder across the back of his throne, ready to be unsheathed at a moment's notice.

"If you're so anxious to know more about me, I could show you how good I am in bed." He smirked. "That's a mystery we can solve right now."

Eww! Was he seriously trying to get out of this by seducing me? I debated playing along just to get information, but I couldn't force myself to do it. The idea of his greasy black hair close to my face, or his bony hands or tight thin lips pressed against my skin made me want to throw up. I shivered at the thought.

"I'll pass, thanks."

His scythe flew from its holder and into his hand. "Then I suggest you rethink confronting me in my private space, or attacking me with false accusations, or soon...I won't be giving you a choice." He slammed the end of his scythe down on the floor, filling the space with a resounding boom then nodded to the door.

I didn't hesitate. I walked past his throne and rushed to the door, desperate to make my escape while I had the chance. I'd have to find another way to look for Garrett that didn't involve me confronting Death himself, and I knew the perfect person to help me do it.

15

I assumed Holli would have returned to the castle by now, but after a few wrong turns down the main hallway, and a couple accidental interruptions, I gave up and walked out the front door. I stood on the bottom step of the massive structure, looking down the street from side-to-side. My palms started to sweat, and the air in my lungs struggled to escape. With Garrett missing, I wasn't exactly sure what to do with myself. I stepped onto the street and began to walk to *Digger's* simply out of habit.

Suddenly, a noise above me snagged my attention.

Yes! Holli was landing on a small balcony high up on the far side of the castle.

I shot into the air, calling out her name. "Holli!" I hovered just beyond the balustrade.

"Hi, Raven. Is there something wrong? Do we have another gathering mission so soon?"

"No, no. I just wanted to see if you'd like to join me for dinner at *Digger's*."

She tilted her head and frowned. "Digger's?"

"Yes, it's a restaurant here in Purgatory." I laughed.

"Really? I didn't realize there were places to eat here. Death always takes me topside for dinner."

Excellent! This was exactly the type of info I needed. If Garrett had discovered Death's dirty little secret, then so could I, even if I had to come at it from a different angle.

"Well, it's a great place, and I'm headed there now if you'd like to join me."

She hesitated, looking back into the small room behind her. "I'm sorry, I would love to go with you, but I'm actually not allowed to leave without Death's permission."

"Are you kidding me?"

"No. As I've told you, you're the only person I get to see." She smiled like the fact didn't bother her in the slightest.

"Doesn't that upset you? I mean, being a *kept* woman?"

The blank look on her face was so innocent it caught me off guard. I could feel my feelings about her shifting, sliding from annoyance to pity.

"Never mind. How about I come in, and we can chat in

your room instead?" I asked.

"Actually, no. You can't come in."

I jerked my chin, her rebuff smacking me in the face.

"Oh no...it's not because I don't want you to. You literally *can't* come in. Death spelled my room and is the only one who can enter."

Wow. What a sick bastard Death was turning out to be.

I opened my mouth—planning to offer another alternative—when the door to her room opened behind her. Death's silhouette filled the space, the invading light spilling around him. I could only imagine the look on his face.

I flared my wings to maintain my position, then took off like a bat out of hell. I wasn't going to push my luck with him any further tonight.

I landed outside of *Digger's* and walked in, rushing to my regular booth in the back. I'd begun to devise my next move when a set of broad shoulders—accompanied by a bad attitude—appeared at my table.

"What the hell's wrong with you? Someone ruffle those precious feathers of yours?"

"Fuck off, Krev."

I hadn't seen the bane of my existence since the last time Garrett and I had gone to the bar.

Garrett.

Thinking of him made it hard to breathe. I sat quietly and

stared at Krev while he appeared to contemplate what his next insult should be.

"Where's your boy toy? I figured since you can't defend yourself, you wouldn't go anywhere without him these days."

There it was. Lame, to the point, and at the moment the perfect thing to say to piss me off.

I leapt from the booth and wrapped my hand around Krev's neck.

"How about you get smart for once in your life and leave me alone?" I snarled.

"Whoa, whoa. Calm down, beautiful. Or were you just looking for a way to get your hands on me?"

"Sure, we'll go with that."

I punched him in the face...repeatedly.

Digger was at my side, grabbing my arm and pulling me back before I could land another hit to Krev's jaw. The feel of my fist against his nose was satisfying but didn't relieve the anger that had built up inside of me.

"Enough!" Death's voice boomed through the room. All the Reapers, including me, stood silent while Digger handed Krev a napkin for his bloodied face.

"Raven. Come with me."

Whispers filled the air and assumptions about my punishment floated through the room. Everyone's eyes were on me as I followed Death out the door.

"I'm sorry, Krev just..."

Death waved his hand to silence my explanation, grabbed my wrist, and teleported us back to his chamber.

Sweat beaded on my skin when he stalked to his throne and retrieved his scythe.

Oh shit!

What was I going to do if he came at me with that damn thing? I wasn't ready for my final death.

I blew out a faint breath when he sat down and placed it across his lap. His cold stare bore into me and an overwhelming desire to spout all my sins overtook me. My mouth opened, but again, he raised his hand for my silence.

"I don't want to hear your excuses. Not about your fight with Krev, or why you accused me of hurting Garrett earlier. What I do want to know is exactly what you said to Holli?"

Damn. How was I going to play this? Defiance was my first instinct, but the pull in my gut and the look on Death's face told me that that would be a mistake. So, I took a deep breath and confessed.

"I didn't say anything to her, really. I just asked if she'd like to join me for dinner. I wasn't aware you had spelled her room or that she couldn't go out without your permission. I'm sorry. With Garrett missing, I felt lonely and thought she and I could spend some time getting to know each other better. That's all."

There...that was mostly the truth.

Silence reigned while he processed my answer. I prayed he didn't have a way to tell if I was lying or not. Finally, the grip on his scythe relaxed.

"Thank you for reaching out to Holli. I know she appreciates it and so do I."

Yeah right, sure you do. A slow smile crept across my face. I lifted my chin and squared my shoulders. "May I ask, why you've decided to keep her separated from the rest of the Reapers?"

"No, you may not."

I nodded and turned to walk away, but Death continued.

"I won't allow Holli to join you for dinner, but I'll modify the spell on her room to grant you access."

"Thank you. I'll visit her tomorrow morning, if that's all right."

"Actually you'll be spending the next two days with her."

My eyes widened.

"I can't have the other Reapers thinking you got off scot-free after your little outburst with Krev. This way you'll get to spend time with Holli, *and* I'll get to keep things in order without anyone being the wiser."

"Thank you?" My response came out more like a question than a statement. I didn't know what else to say. On one hand I just got a two-day girl's retreat with the one person who had inside details about Death; on the other, I just got punished with a two-day lockdown with Death's girlfriend. *Yay me!*

He rose from his throne, scythe in hand, and gestured for me to follow him. We walked through the main halls of the castle, catching as many eyes as possible. Once we reached the passage that led to the dungeons, the whispers of my punishment had grown wildly, exactly as Death had planned, no doubt. He dismissed the stragglers and waited until we were alone before reaching for my arm.

We reappeared outside a small door in a thin, empty hallway. He motioned for me to stand aside, then placed the tip of his weapon against the wood. His chest rumbled when he began chanting under his breath. The tip of cold metal flared with a sudden burst, revealing hidden sigils that were magically etched all over the entrance to Holli's room. As they faded, Death removed the scythe then turned to me and smiled.

"You're now able to enter the room, but due to your punishment, you can't leave until I release you."

My breath hitched. *Well, that's not good.*

16

Holli beamed as we entered her room. In two seconds flat she was in Death's arms, thanking him for allowing me to come visit her. His eyes caught mine over her shoulder, and I assumed the serious lift to his brow indicated I was supposed to keep my mouth shut.

"You're welcome, my sweet. I thought the two of you could spend the weekend together."

I cringed, her squeal piercing my eardrums.

Death continued, effectively cutting off any questions Holli was about to pose. "Food, drink, and entertainment will be provided for you here, and there shouldn't be any outbreaks so neither of you will have to worry about leaving."

I practically had to bite my tongue to stop myself from

asking exactly how he knew that. But again, the stern look he shot in my direction made it clear I needed to keep my mouth shut.

My nostrils flared, and I could feel my inner light starting to build. My anger was rising, and I was in serious need of a distraction.

I turned to take in the tiny room and quickly wondered how I was going to survive the next two days trapped within these cold stone walls. I was suddenly very grateful for my modern apartment and all the conveniences it provided, because living in a castle like this was something I would never be able to do.

Already stifled, I moved towards the balcony. I looked out over Purgatory and my insides tightened.

Where are you, Garrett?

I was still sure Death had something to do with his disappearance, but was now confused by the fact that he'd just shut me in with the one person I was certain could spill his secrets. Maybe he didn't have anything to hide after all. Nevertheless, I planned on spending my "punishment" hunting for information.

"Raven, I'll have Drey send over some of your clothes."

I spun around, tilted my head and smirked. "Thank you. That will be great."

Death placed a kiss on the back of Holli's hand before

leaving the room. The instant the door was shut she spun around and skipped in my direction. I smiled and shrugged. I wasn't sure what to say or do next, but luckily, Holli wasn't afflicted with my shyness and began to babble incessantly.

I learned how much she loved being Death's "personal" Reaper, as she put it, along with the fact that despite my disgust, she and Death were involved and apparently he was a decent lover. *Gag. Was I missing something?* I couldn't understand how someone as beautiful as Holli could be attracted so someone as revolting as Death. We were only three hours into my sentence, and I already wanted to scratch out my eyes and rip off my ears. *Heaven save me.* I jumped up from my seated position on the bed and began to pace, desperate to change the subject to something far less personal and disturbing.

"Do you like living here? In Death's castle, I mean?"

"Yes. I absolutely love it."

I involuntarily scrunched up my nose. *How in the hell could she love it here?*

Holli must have sensed my confusion because her knowing smile became almost sympathetic. She didn't say another word but walked towards a section of the wall where a tapestry hung from ceiling to floor. When she pushed it aside, the wall was the same gray stone but appeared to have a lucidity about it.

"I want to show you something," she said.

With a light touch of her fingertips, a portal shimmered and became a doorway. The long hallway I saw beyond the molten wall looked bright and welcoming.

"Let's go." Holli walked through the mercurial substance and merged into the scene beyond.

I stepped through, following her lead.

"*This* is where I live," she explained, like I was supposed to understand.

"What is this place?" *Where is this place?*

"Death created it for me. It's an extension of the castle but exists in an alternate dimension. No one in Purgatory can see it or sense it, and no one but me, Death, and now you have ever been to it."

My heart leapt, knowing I'd just hit the jackpot. "Why would you need an entire castle in a different dimension to live in? Why couldn't you just live in Death's castle like normal?"

"I don't know. Death just said that he wanted a place where we wouldn't be watched and where I could be safe."

Eww. That sounded sexual and gross, and possibly ominous. Why would Holli need to be kept safe?

I halted the barrage of questions flooding my brain and looked around at the structure. I needed to find a clue as to why this place existed. The hall was tiled with white marble and the walls were made mostly of glass. The view beyond them was that of Purgatory, but seen as if you were looking at a watercolor. No grays and blacks, but instead reds, blues, and purples all smeared together like a Monet painting.

Holli beckoned me to follow her and I did, eyes wide and ears open. We continued for a short stint, then turned into a large room. The area was enormous and had a high ceiling that featured a massive tangle of thin metal beams that twisted and seemed to creep up the walls, coming to an inverted point that hung down towards the floor.

"Wow. What is that?"

"Oh, that's where Death pulls the phenoms inside."

My jaw dropped. "What do you mean? Why would he need a way to pull them inside?" My tone was far too demanding, and Holli paused before responding.

"Um...I'm not sure if I'm suppose to tell you or not." She started to turn away, heading back towards the hallway that led to the portal.

"Wait. Holli, I'm sorry. I didn't mean to pry. I'm just so surprised at the grandeur of this place. It's so beautiful. You're lucky to be able to live here."

Holli lifted her chin and shifted her shoulders, her proud smile evidence that I said the right thing.

"Thanks. It's not as big as Death's actual castle, but it has a lot of fun things for me to do when I'm not working with you."

I shook my head and struggled to maintain the smile I'd plastered onto my face. Using the words "Death" and "fun" in the same sentence went against the natural order of things. Then again, I wasn't the girlfriend he was trying to impress. Maybe Death pulled the phenoms inside for Holli to fly with— this room was certainly big enough for her to do so, and that was certainly something *I* considered fun.

"Would you like to see the gardens?" she asked.

"Absolutely!" *Flowers? In Purgatory? This I had to see.* My mind rejoiced at the prospect and my smile turned genuine. I hadn't touched or smelled a real flower since before I died.

We walked away from the "Phenom Room," and continued down the hallway towards another section of Holli's castle.

The level of kindness that Death had shown her boggled my mind. I couldn't imagine the amount of magic it took to pull off something like this. I swallowed hard as a sinking feeling settled in my gut.

I knew all of this was somehow related to the increased number of phenoms and Garrett's disappearance. Now, if I could only figure out how they were connected.

"So, Holli. You said that Death takes you topside for dinner every night. What is your favorite place to eat?"

"Oh wow. That's a tough question. We've been to so many great places. Le Meurice in Paris was amazing, but I also really enjoyed Antoine's in New Orleans."

Dammit. I refused to let the green-eyed monster rear his head, but I'd never been to either of those places when I was alive, let alone once I was dead.

"I've been wanting to go to back to the French Quarter, perhaps I could ask Death to take us both there tomorrow tonight."

A wide smile layered my expression and my excitement rivaled hers. "That would be fantastic!"

Now, maybe I'd get some answers.

17

We didn't see Death again for the remainder of the night, and when Holli had tried to go find him to discuss our dinner plans, we found that she too was unable to leave the room.

No surprise I suppose.

After wriggling the door back and forth for at least a full minute, the innocent shrug of her shoulders portrayed a habit of accepting odd things without a second thought. Something I'd NEVER be able to do.

"Hmm. I guess Death wants us to stay in." She gazed toward the balcony, which was also blocked by an invisible barrier.

"Clearly," I responded, flopping down on the bed. "Holli, can I ask you something?"

"Sure."

"Do you know why there has been such an increase in phenoms lately? I mean, there have always been a few that figure out a way to run, but nothing like what's been happening since your arrival." I was sick of getting nowhere and figured I might as well just ask.

"I'm not sure, Raven. Like I explained before, Death told me that my only job here was to help you gather the phenoms, and protect him whenever necessary." The crease to her brow made it obvious she didn't like being blamed for something she didn't understand.

"I'm sorry. I wasn't trying to imply it's your fault. It's just confusing to me, is all."

Holli didn't respond, but turned back towards the balcony, flaring her snow-white wings ever so slightly. I needed to tread lightly here. If Holli got mad, all it would take was one word from her, and I would end up in the dungeons for real. "Don't worry about it," I offered.

Her shoulders slumped, and she blew out a shallow breath. I couldn't quite decipher if this was her way of relaxing because she truly didn't know anything, or if it meant that, in fact, she did.

I was almost grateful when Death opened the door, disrupting our awkward exchange. Holli smiled at him, but it didn't quite reach her eyes.

"What's wrong, my dear?" he asked, his gaze shifting to me.

I swallowed hard when Holli squinted in my direction.

"Nothing. I was just trying to come find you to ask if we could take Raven to the French Quarter for dinner and found that I couldn't leave my room."

"I'm sorry, darling. Raven isn't allowed topside unless she is on a retrieval or gathering mission."

"Oh, all right. Forgive me, I didn't know." Her voice was timid but held an edge.

Death leaned down and kissed Holli on the cheek while his eyes remained glued to mine. "It was nice of you to want to include her."

He pulled back and smiled down at Holli, then pulled her to the edge of the room. With a swipe of his scythe, a small round table dressed in white linen and surrounded by three wooden chairs appeared out of thin air. Holli squealed, and I could only assume it was a table setting from Antoine's restaurant.

"Will this do, my love?" Death asked Holli.

"Oh yes. This is wonderful. Thank you so much." Her giddy response pulled a wide smile from his lips.

He motioned for us to take a seat then uncovered the silver domed serving dishes to reveal our Southern cuisine. My mouth watered as I took it all in. We enjoyed an appetizer of Huitres Thermidor; a plate of fresh Louisiana oysters baked on the half shell with a bacon and tomato sauce. The main entrée was Cotelettes d'agneau grillées; a prime center cut lamb chops grilled and served with mint jelly. Dessert, of course, was the highlight. The Omelette Alaska Antoine was a special presentation of baked Alaska and something I would never forget. I closed my eyes letting the meringue, cake, and ice cream melt on my tongue.

"Are you enjoying your meal, Raven?"

I opened my eyes to Death's hungry stare. I straightened my spine and lifted my chin. "Yes. Thank you. It was delicious," I stated flatly.

Death's sneer was hidden from Holli's view.

What did he expect? For me to fall for this lame attempt to seduce me into some kinky three-way with an intimate dinner and good food? *Hell no!* Besides, he should be used to my rejections by now. Or, maybe he was just rubbing my face in all the extravagance I'd missed out on by turning him down all those times. *Oh well!*

"I'm glad to hear it," Death replied. "Also, I have news that I think will interest you."

I tilted my head and let a fake smile rest upon my lips.

"I saw Garrett today. He was walking back from that donut shop you two like to frequent. He seemed to be lost in thought but healthy enough. Be sure to ask him about his disappearance when you leave here tomorrow night; I'll be interested to hear what he has to say."

My inner light started to build, and I clenched my fists.

Son of a bitch!

This asshole certainly knew a thing or two about torture; it was going to kill me not to be able to reach Garrett for another twenty-four hours. Looks like Death won this tête-à-tête after all.

"Thanks for the information. I'll be sure to do just that." My tone was sharp, and I couldn't care less. Death could explain to Holli why this bit of news upset me so much; I was done playing house with the odd couple from Hell.

I'd forced myself to lay down and sleep the moment Death magically cleared the remnants of our glorious feast and bid Holli goodnight with a disgustingly passionate kiss. It was no surprise when that kiss and her never-ending giggles became a recurring theme in my nightmare.

Today, I'd asked Holli for some time alone, giving her the excuse that I was worried about Garrett. Thankfully, she didn't pry, and I was able to spend the day walking through the gardens of her fake fairytale castle.

By the time I'd wandered through the maze of roses, tulips, and my favorites—peonies, I'd started to feel a bit better. Which, of course, was the perfect time for Death to make an appearance.

"What do you think of the home I've created for Holli?"

I didn't hesitate in my response. "It's lovely, but I don't understand the need for it. If you'd just let her mingle with the rest of the Reapers, this entire ruse wouldn't be necessary. What is it that you're really trying to hide?"

The edge of his thin lip twitched, and I knew I'd struck a chord.

"Do you think I'd let you stay with Holli and wander around here if I had anything to hide?"

That was the million dollar question, wasn't it? And by him saying those words out loud, it was also the answer. Yes. Death did have something to hide, and it was evident by how hard he was trying to prove otherwise.

"Do you want to tell me about the Phenom Room?" I inquired.

"The what?" he asked, his tone amused.

"The room where you pull the phenoms inside."

"It's simply so Holli can practice her flying. She enjoys having something to interact with during her training."

"That brings up another question. Why train her to fight? And what in the world could a tiny little girl protect the almighty Death from?"

The air between us vibrated just before Death struck me across the face.

I grabbed my cheek, stunned, then flared my wings and prepared to defend myself.

"There. Now you look like you've spent two days being punished for your crime. Go home, Raven. I'm sure Garrett is waiting for you with bated breath."

Death disappeared before I could respond.

When I pushed back through the portal, Holli was waiting outside on the balcony. "Looks like we can get out of the room now," she said as I joined her.

"Yes. Death has instructed me it's time I return home."

Holli turned in my direction, her eyes widening at the site of my blossoming black eye, no doubt. The fact that she didn't say anything spoke volumes. She reached out and hugged me. I allowed it, but reciprocated in half-measures, wrapping my one arm around her shoulders and giving them a slight squeeze. "See you back on the job, I guess," I offered.

"Yes, I guess so. And I hope Garrett's okay."

"Thanks." I gathered my things and reached to open the door. It was still locked. I turned back to Holli and shrugged. She smiled and gestured to the balcony.

I waved goodbye and took to the sky. As I looked back, I couldn't deny that my feelings towards her had softened slightly, but that didn't change the fact that she was still my number one source for information.

Sorry, Holli, but thanks for the info.

18

The instant I glided through my window I knew Garrett was waiting inside. How he got there, however, I wasn't sure since my door was still locked from when I'd left before.

I threw my things on the bed and raced into the living room. He was sitting on the couch, his smile like the breaking dawn after a long winter's night, warming me and bringing tears to my eyes. When he saw my face, however, things got serious. "What the hell happened to you?" he demanded.

What happened to me? He was the one who passed out, got sick, then disappeared.

"Death happened. What about you? Are you okay? Where did he take you?" I moved to sit on the coffee table in front of him.

He squinted and got that cute grin he always wore when he was confused. "I'm not sure what you mean. Death didn't do anything to me."

Hmph. Maybe Death erased his memory. *Was that even possible?*

"What's the last thing you remember?" I pried.

"Well, I remember closing shop on Friday, then heading to *Digger's* to grab some food for us. After that, it's a bit of a blur. But when I woke up, it was Saturday afternoon, and I was here...in your bed." He wiggled his eyebrows, teasing at the implication of his words.

"As if." I laughed and threw myself into his arms for a quick hug. "Well, I for one think Death is totally fucking with us. When you didn't show up for our meeting Friday night, I flew out to find you and you were laid out on the road, surrounded by Reapers. I brought you back here when your fever spiked, but before I could help you, you disappeared."

"Seriously?" He stood up and started pacing. "Wow. I don't remember anything like that. After I woke up here, I grabbed your spare key from the credenza, went to get some donuts, and headed to my house to clean up. I came back this afternoon and let myself in. Figured I'd wait for you to get back from whatever gathering mission you were on." He scrubbed his hand over his head. "I seriously passed out in front of a bunch of Reapers? Who?"

"Shit, I don't remember. Peters was there, Richardson, Monamoa, and I think Levine and maybe Crawley."

Garrett lost all color in his face and flopped back down on the couch. "What do you think happened to me? You said I had a fever...how's that even possible."

"That's what I'm saying. I think Death did this and erased your memory. Who else could hurt you and cause you to simply disappear into thin air?"

Garrett's eyes snapped to mine.

"What?" I demanded.

"Nothing. Just let it go, okay?"

"Um...no. I won't just let it go. What aren't you telling me?"

"Do you remember when I said I thought I had an idea and that if I was right it would be really bad?" he rambled.

"Yes."

"Well, I think I'm right, and it's definitely really bad. So bad, they took the memories of what I found out."

"They? Who are you talking about?"

Garrett looked around the room, raising his eyes to the ceiling.

"Garrett, tell me!"

"I can't."

I jumped up, flexing my fingers, ready to punch something until I got answers. I couldn't believe that Garrett had information but was choosing to leave me in the dark.

"Why won't you tell me? I can handle it. I swear."

"No. Raven. You can't. That's what I'm trying to say. Leave it be. Just do your job and let things lie."

What the hell is wrong with him? It wasn't like Garrett to give up when there was a bread crumb to follow. And now, with the introduction of some mysterious "they," I was surprised he wasn't racing out my front door and straight to Death's castle to hound him for answers right this very second.

I placed my hands on the bricks of the fireplace and let my head drop. I needed to calm down, but apparently that wasn't in the cards. My wings flared, knocking a vase off the mantle. I was pissed and there was no hiding it. When my inner light reached its peak, Garrett rushed forward and grabbed me. We were both catapulted through space, arriving in Heaven seconds later.

"*That's* why I couldn't tell you. I knew you wouldn't be able to come here without getting pissed off and igniting your inner light." Garrett's tone was excited and rang with a cocky, I-told-you-so, vibe.

I looked around the white expanse, shocked that this was his intended destination. "Oh."

"You asked who else could hurt me and make me disappear?" He gestured towards the golden gates of Heaven. "Well...here you go!"

"No way! Are you telling me Heaven has somehow become involved with whatever secret Death is keeping and you figured it out?"

"I'm not sure, but that is the only thing that makes sense. Plus, I have this nagging feeling of feathers tickling me in unmentionable places," he joked.

I laughed out loud.

"Okay. We're here, so who do we talk to?"

"Me." A booming voice echoed behind us.

I spun around to see an *extremely* large male angel stalking in our direction. A chill ran through me when I saw the sword in his hand, but it was the thick muscles and bronzed skin peeking out from under his robe that did me in.

He was gorgeous. Dark hair, pure white wings, and violet-blue eyes—he radiated warmth as if he'd been formed from a piece of the sun.

Wow! Am I drooling?

Yep. I sure was.

"My name is Michael, and I'm surprised to see you both here." He looked between the two of us and after leveling me with his gaze, turned back to Garrett. "I thought the block we put on your mind would have remained in place better than this."

"So I was right, Heaven is involved," Garrett remarked.

"Yes. There are things at work that neither of you can be privy to. The knowledge could affect the outcome and we cannot veer off course. Death has forced our hand, and we are fighting back, but it's imperative that he not learn of our involvement." He paused to look in my direction again, effectively making my knees go weak. "Raven, you're very important, so I need to ask that you do as Garrett instructed and just let things lie. Your time will come, and all will be revealed."

He reached out to stroke my cheek. I closed my eyes and let my head lull to the side, pressing into his hand. I'd basically become a bobble-head doll, melting at this man's touch. *What the heck?*

Garrett coughed into his fist while trying—but failing—to hide his smile. "We won't say a word."

Michael turned and nodded in Garrett's direction, but didn't remove his hand from my face. When he looked back at me, his gaze pierced my soul.

We were locked in some strange emotional pull, unspoken, but completely intense. I couldn't move. I wondered if he saw me as a simple girl—a tool to use in his heavenly plan, or was it the woman he'd aroused within me that had captured his attention?

My question was answered when he leaned down, bringing his mouth to mine. The soft pressure sent tiny sparks into my lips, plumping them just for him. My body moved closer of its own accord—my brain completely detached from the motion. Michael never hesitated. He pulled me close, wrapping his arm around my lower back and increased the intensity of our kiss. By the time he set me back on the ground, I had to work to untangle my hands from his hair.

"I'll be in touch," was all he said before a bright light burst, and Michael disappeared.

Garrett and I stood, staring at one another, then his boisterous laugh filled the space between us. "Oh my God...you just made out with the Archangel Michael," Garrett exclaimed.

I opened my mouth to respond but was instead sent plummeting back through space and into my living room.

"Raven. Are you okay?" Garrett's voice sounded strained.

"Yes. I think so. What happened?" I asked, completely confused as to why I was lying on the floor.

"I'm not sure, but this is the second time I've woken up in your apartment without any idea of how I got here."

19

After conducting a full-scale interrogation on each other, we decided there wasn't anything left to do but get back to our normal routines. No matter how hard we tried, we were only left with more questions as to what had happened and how we'd both ended up on the floor, completely dazed and confused.

The work week had started, and I was on duty again. The familiarity felt good, and I used it as sort of a meditation.

I stood in a stark hospital room, waiting for my next retrieval, and let memories of my human life flood my mind. I'd made my career out of caring for the sick, so to now be the one who escorted them to their final destinies was nothing less than a gift. As much as I disliked Death, I was still honored by the position he'd given me.

The young boy who'd lost his battle with cancer lay covered by a thin sheet. His parents sobbed, struggling to say their final goodbyes. I brushed the back of my hand over my cheeks, trying to stop the free-flow of tears. This was something I'd witnessed again and again, but it was always difficult when the soul was that of a child.

Just before the young man's spirit lifted from his body, I began to witness highlights of his short life. The first memory was that of his mother and father in a loving embrace. The second was that of his sister graduating high school, a proud smile on her face. The third and final was that of the doctors and nurses who'd helped him deal with his illness, their kind faces and loving hearts impacting the boy's psyche. I took his hand when his soul emerged and repeated my usual phrase. "Please don't fear me. I'm only here to help you find peace."

His joyous smile filled my heart, and suddenly, I could no longer breathe.

Literally.

I tried to inhale but couldn't. My lungs were already filled to capacity. Within seconds I was on the verge of panic but finally forced myself to exhale.

A thick thread of white smoke escaped my lips and entered the boy's mouth. His eyes grew wide.

The foggy substance continued to flow into him, and I felt his spirit pull away from me. I prepared to throw out my Reaper ribbons to keep him from running, but before they fully extended, the young man's soul returned to his physical body.

I stared, my mouth agape.

His body began to glow from the inside out, expelling the same pearly white mist out his pores—the mist he'd ingested from me.

I took a step forward, hovering over the hospital bed to get a closer look. His chest began to rise, and color flooded his cheeks.

He took a breath.

The machines went wild, and I went blank. *What the HELL is happening?*

Doctors and nurses raced into the room, while the boy's parents were forced to gather outside the door. I watched the chaos, my thoughts a swirl of wonderful impossibilities. When the machines fell silent, and the final order had been shouted, the boy's parents rushed forward, embracing their newly revived son in a flurry of prayers and tears.

Hell had nothing to do with this; this was a freakin' miracle.

20

I paced Garrett's apartment, waiting for him to dismiss the last two Reapers and lock the door. The second he opened the night drop with a wave of his hand, I started in. "Garrett! I'm telling you I just brought a kid back to life. As in, I literally breathed life *into* him."

"What in the world are you talking about, Raven? He was just probably another white-lighter."

White-lighters were people who died for a brief moment, which afforded them the chance to see the *white-light* before returning to their bodies. It happened occasionally, but not very often.

"No. He wasn't a white-lighter. He actually came to me, but instead of my light building to open the portal, my lungs were filled with a weird cloudy mist that came out my mouth and flowed into his. It filled him up, then he returned to his body and Came. Back. To. Life." I stressed each of my last words.

Garrett never stopped scribbling, tallying the days counts.

"Garrett!!" I slammed my hand down on his desk. "I'm serious. Something strange is happening to me."

Garrett dropped his pen and looked up. "Raven, relax. If something is happening to you, it's probably just another new perk."

"I don't think so. I know something's up, but I'm not sure it has anything to do with Death." I began to pace his study again, taking a brief moment to randomly ponder how his rug stayed in such good shape with all the traffic it saw. "I'm not even sure my dreams *are* a perk. I've never talked to him about it, and he's never brought it up."

"Maybe you should just ask him," Garrett rationalized.

I shook my head, contemplating the suggestion. "I don't think so. I have this weird feeling that my dreams and now this 'mist thing' are somehow connected. I just need to figure out how."

"Sounds like a plan. Are you still keeping your dream journal?" Garrett asked.

I lowered my head. "No."

"Well, maybe you should start again, because if the two

things are related, it may be the only way to figure out how or why you have these new 'abilities' and where they came from."

He was right. I'd need to start keeping track of the faces I saw in my dreams and notate the events that happened during their retrievals.

Three days passed before I was able to write something interesting in my journal. I'd seen plenty of faces in my dreams, yet their retrievals were nothing like the miracle boy's—until today.

Last night, I'd dreamt of an old man, and when we'd come face-to-face, his elderly gaze was as peaceful as the memories of his life that played across my mind. When I'd reached for his outstretched hand, I felt the familiar tug that indicated the mist in my lungs had started to build. Sure enough, when I tried to breathe in, I couldn't. Then, just like last time, I exhaled, and the cloudy substance flowed from me to him in a steady stream. I moved closer, placing my hand on his face, mesmerized while the last filaments of vapor entered his mouth.

His soul returned to his body, and the steamy light radiated through his pores from the inside out. He took a new breath and opened his eyes. He'd searched the room for me but found nothing, for he was no longer in the netherworld, but once again truly alive.

I closed my journal but remained in the memory, trying to focus on anything that was similar about the two incidents. Nothing stood out, but then again, each time I'd been so overwhelmed and left with such a benevolent feeling, I could hardly keep a linear thought in my head. I'd have to try harder next time—if there was a next time—to make sure I cataloged more details.

A noise caught my attention from just beyond my bedroom window. I glanced up and spotted Holli hovering outside.

"Another round of breakouts has occurred. It's time to go." Her formality caught me off guard. I dove out the window, and we headed for the portal fields.

"How have you been?" I asked, happy to see her again, even if it was under the guise of work.

"I'm well, thank you. And yourself?"

I glanced in her direction and found the muscles in her jaw were as tight as her words. "What's wrong, Holli?"

"Nothing. Why do you ask?" The twitch of her head and the increased grinding of her teeth made it obvious she was lying.

"Because, I can tell something is bothering you."

She stole a glance in my direction; the frown she wore and the flare to her nose made her features look pouty with a hint of disgust.

"Geez, what's with the look?"

We landed in front of portal 221, and before I could press her for an answer, I received a quick smack to the face.

My hand flew to my cheek. "Ouch. What the hell was that for?"

"Do you think I don't know?!" she yelled.

"Know what?"

"You tried to steal Death away from me that day in the garden!"

My mouth fell open. If anyone wanted to attack me right now, they would have succeeded. I was in shock, utterly stunned, and the ability to speak or act was completely beyond my grasp.

"That's why he hit you. He told me all about it. Once you saw my castle you were so jealous that you tried to steal him away by throwing yourself at him. He had to hit you to snap you out of it."

Oh.My.GOD! What game was he playing at? One minute he wanted us to be great pals, the next he was setting us up to throw down.

"Holli, I'm not sure why Death told you that story, but that's exactly what it is...A. Story. I would never try to steal

Death from you. If I wanted to be his girlfriend, I would have just said yes all those times he asked me before you were even here."

That earned me another slap across the face. My intention was to make her understand that I'd *never* had an interest in Death, now or before her arrival. But apparently that's not how it came across.

"He said you'd say that. But now that you see the things he gives me and how much he cares for me, you changed your mind."

"This is ridiculous," I bellowed. "Call him here right now. Let's see what he has to say when confronted with us both."

Hollie stilled. The fact that I was willing to argue my point in front of them both must have broken through the thick lie layering her brain. Her shoulders slumped and her lips began to quiver. "I'm not sure which bothers me more. The idea of my only friend hurting me, or my lover constantly lying to me." The dam released and tears raced down her cheeks.

Oh man. I was not good at this girly shit. And even though I felt bad playing the 'you-can-count-on-me' card to find out what Death had been lying about, I couldn't really pass up the opportunity.

I strode forward and placed a hand on her shoulder. "I'm sorry, Holli. But please know, I would never do anything to hurt you on purpose." I added that last part in case Death's secret somehow involved her, which meant she wouldn't remain unscathed once it was revealed. "Now, besides this whopper about me being a boyfriend stealer, what else has Death been lying to you about?"

I wasn't sure if she'd answer a direct question, but figured it couldn't hurt to ask.

"Recently, he's been leaving me alone a lot more, and when I asked him why, he said it was to test a theory. I didn't know what he meant so I kept asking. He told me to drop it or he'd cut me off from my castle." Sobs shook her petite form. "He's never treated me like that before, and I know it has something to do with the phenoms he keeps pulling inside."

My ears perked up. "I thought he did that just so you could practice flying?"

"I thought so too, but now, he won't even let me practice or be in there at all when he does it." She buried her head in her hands.

I continued to pat her on the shoulder, offering what condolences I could. I tried to imagine what theory Death could be testing and how it involved the phenoms.

My mind was humming, then Holli straightened and wiped her tears. The resolved look on her face made me nervous. "If Death wants to keep experimenting with the phenoms that *we* gather, I wonder what he'd do if we simply refused?"

Oh shit! Holli was turning out to be braver than I imagined, but disobeying Death was not an option unless you were ready to face his scythe. Maybe he hadn't explained those things to her because she was his girlfriend. However, I didn't think that fact made her immune from his anger if she decided to test his authority. "Holli, that's not a good idea. Death will deliver the final death to any Reaper who doesn't do as instructed. I've seen it done and personally, I'm not ready to die."

She huffed a hard breath, turned to portal 221, and walked inside. I wasn't sure if I'd dissuaded her rebellion, but for her sake and mine, I certainly hoped so.

21

I followed Holli through the portal, emerging in Egypt, the pyramids standing clearly in the distance.

"Wow. I've never been to Africa before," I stated, trying to engage her in a less stressful conversation.

It didn't work.

She remained silent and flew toward a cloud of buzzing phenoms. I shut my mouth and hung back, waiting for her to raise her sword like normal. My eyes bugged out when she flew directly into the center of the swirling mass instead.

"Holli!" I shouted. *What the hell is she doing?*

The cloud began to thin.

Holli was wielding The Devourer as if it were an extension of her body. She cut and sliced through the phenoms, sucking them into her glowing weapon with each hack. Her intensity shocked me. I realized I was getting a front row demonstration of Death's "personal" Reaper. Her training meant to protect him was evident in each lethal blow.

"Holli, calm down."

"Why? Am I not allowed to get angry when someone lies to me?"

"Of course you are, but taking it out on the phenoms isn't going to get you anywhere."

Her eyes narrowed. I worried for a second she was going to turn her fury towards me, but luckily, she sighed and lowered her sword. I watched the last phenom get sucked into the weapon, its wispy tail slithering across the ground.

"It doesn't hurt them, you know." She took a deep breath, and a smile crept across her lips. "But it does make me feel better."

We both laughed at her tantrum and finished the mission with our spirits lifted. By the time we exited the mausoleum back in the portal fields, our cheeks were sore and Holli's anger had dissipated.

"Thanks for making me feel better, Raven. I guess if Death needs to keep something from me he probably has a very good reason."

And, there it was...that unwavering innocence that always amazed me. "Holli, you're a very special person. I'm sorry if I was hard on you initially."

"Why do you say that? You've always been kind to me," Holli responded.

I scoffed internally. If she only knew the hateful things that had gone through my mind and flitted across my tongue. I shook my head, admitting to myself I actually liked this girl. "Let's just say, I'm glad I've had the chance to get to know you. You're a big help, and I'm happy to call you my friend."

Tears began to shine in her eyes. I still wasn't comfortable with the whole "BFF" thing, but I was trying. She launched herself at me with her arms flung wide. I embraced her fully, laughing as we stumbled off-balance.

"Well, well...isn't this cute." Krev's voice sliced through the air.

I spun around, instinctively shielding Holli behind me. "What do you want, Krev?"

He gestured over my shoulder at Holli. "I just came to meet this beauty."

My eyes widened.

What the hell?

How could Krev see her when no one else could? Maybe Death had lifted his magical shroud and simply hadn't told us about it.

Krev took a step towards us, halting my internal debate. I reached back and grabbed Holli's hand, preparing to propel us both into the sky but was halted when Duncan, another Reaper, stepped out from the mausoleum behind us and grabbed her other arm.

I spun, ready to launch a kick to his midsection but stumbled when I realized my services weren't required.

A chill layered the air, then Holli had Duncan on the ground, her sword poised at his neck. She looked at me and shrugged, obviously surprised by the change in her situation as well.

Krev threw up his hands in mock defeat. "Whoa, hold on there, beautiful. We only wanted to introduce ourselves and have the pleasure of meeting the newest female Reaper."

I rolled my eyes, sickened by his typical rhetoric, but Holli remained silent; stoic and deadly. Neither of the guys had a clue what to do, and I frickin' loved it. Innocent or not, Holli was a badass.

"Well, sorry, Krev, but I don't think she has any interest in meeting you," I stated flatly.

His nostrils flared and his upper lip curled, but before he could move or respond, Death appeared, coalescing out of thin air and black smoke.

"Do we have a problem here, my dear?" he asked Holli, his voice smooth as silk, but deadly nonetheless.

"No problem at all, my love," Holli responded as if nothing was amiss.

The look of fear and utter confusion on the boys' faces sent me spiraling into a fit of laughter. Everyone looked in my direction.

"What's so funny?" Krev demanded.

"Actually, you guys are," I chided. "You should see the looks on your faces. Here's this little waif of a girl who just went all ninja on Duncan's ass, and you've got Death breathing down your neck for messing with his woman." I doubled over, laughing so hard I could barely breathe. "Finally...someone else is in trouble besides me."

Krev and Duncan didn't find my explanation very funny, but Holli and Death both grinned. Death waved his hand in Holli's direction and she immediately withdrew her sword from Duncan's neck. He popped upright and shuffled away as fast as he could.

Death turned to Krev.

"If I wanted to introduce you to the newest addition to our family, I would have done so by now. So I would suggest, the next time your curiosity peaks...fight it."

Krev gave Death a clipped nod and walked away.

Death's gaze slid to me. "Thank you for watching over Holli."

"Are you kidding me? She certainly doesn't need my help. She was ready to take those guys out." I smiled at Holli, noticing her reddened cheeks.

"Regardless of her skills, I'm happy to know you actually have her back." He reached out his arm and enfolded her into his embrace.

I so desperately wanted to spew all the questions running through my mind: How were Krev and Duncan able to see Holli? Why did he lie to Holli about me? What was this theory he was testing, and why couldn't he share it with his Reapers? But, with the mutual peace we all seemed to be experiencing, I quickly decided against it. I'd leave it up to Holli to root out the truth of it all if she still wanted to.

I turned to take my leave, disappointed but resolved, when Death's firm grip settled on my arm. When I spun around, the serious look on his face caused my internal alarms to sound.

"Raven, when was the last time you were sent to Heaven during a retrieval?" His voice was strained and taut.

I pulled from his grasp and took a quick step back, contemplating the odd question. It wasn't unusual for me to visit Heaven, or Hell for that matter; it was part of my job.

"Earlier today, why?"

His jaw clenched, then he and Holli disappeared. *Wow. Guess I won't be getting an answer.*

I shook my head and took to the sky, finally heading home for the night. As I neared my apartment, I saw Garrett rushing up to the main door of my building. I adjusted my trajectory and touched down gently behind him.

"Hey! Fancy meeting you here."

"Actually, it's not fancy at all." His intensity shook me. "I need to talk to you."

"What's wrong?"

"Let's get inside." He ushered me into the building and up the stairs to my apartment with the urgency of an undercover spy on a mission.

I flipped the lock. He unceremoniously pushed me inside, slammed the door, spun me around, and pressed my back against it.

"What are you doing?" I demanded. "I need to check for something." He brushed the hair away from my neck and turned my head from side to side. *This is awkward.* "Garrett, seriously, what the hell is this about?"

"Not *Hell.*"

"What?"

"Hold still." The edge of panic in his voice had my heart racing. He continued to run his thumb over the smooth skin behind my ears and down each side of my neck. "Oh my God, he was right," Garrett breathed.

I'd had enough. I shoved him off with enough force to push him away from me. "What are you talking about?"

"You've been marked, Raven."

I stared at Garrett like he was an idiot, but it was I who was completely clueless. "Marked? By what? What do you mean?"

"I mean..." He grabbed my arm and pulled me to the mirror hanging next to the front door.

"...Heaven has marked you."

22

I gazed at my reflection and focused on the spot he was pointing to. I had to squint, but there, behind my right ear, was a small raised symbol. It looked like a sigil, or rune of some sort, made up of lines, dots and squiggles. Its meaning was completely lost on me.

I spun to face Garrett. "What does this mean?" I demanded.

"It means you're an emissary of Heaven."

My mouth fell open. The look on his face and the hole through my heart became instant twins.

This had to be a mistake. No way could a Reaper of Death be an emissary of Heaven. It simply wasn't possible. *Was it?*

I turned back to the mirror for a second look. I stepped closer, keeping my eyes locked on the symbol. Tears welled in my eyes as it grew larger in the reflection. I backed away and turned to Garrett once more.

"Explain this to me. Am I going to lose my job? Get kicked out of Purgatory?"

Garrett grabbed my hand and led me to the couch. "Sit down, Raven. Just try to relax."

Relax? How could he say that? "Please, just tell me what caused this and what's going to happen to me?"

Garrett took a deep breath. He looked like a preacher about to give a sermon, or a history professor about to deliver a lecture. "I'm not sure, Raven, but there's only been one other Reaper in history who was marked by Heaven."

"Who?"

"Death, but he was also marked by Hell."

My heart clenched.

Beyond what I'd come to know from being his employee, I'd never given much thought to Death or his *life*.

"Go on," I pleaded.

Garrett sighed. "Death was the original Reaper, placed in the position by both Heaven and Hell, and granted the power to rule Purgatory. The two realms struck a covenant that outlined the rules and guidelines that molded his position and that of his Reapers. They marked him as a mutual emissary, since the job he'd hold would serve them both."

I sat silent, his explanation making sense so far.

"Think of the covenant as a binding magical job description. It's why the Reapers are bound by free will and dress the way they do, in their typical 'Reaper' cloaks. It's also how they are chosen and brought to Purgatory. All of this has happened automatically for...well, ever. Until you."

I swallowed hard against the lump in my throat.

"You're an anomaly, Raven. You, and now Holli, are the only Reapers who've been created outside of the covenant." Garrett shook his head. "I wasn't sure how he'd done it or why, but once you got here and started performing like a regular Reaper and we became friends, I didn't think much else about it."

"And what do you think about it now?" I asked, biting my lip.

"I'm not sure. Your numbers have shown that you've been visiting Heaven a lot more often than Hell lately. Maybe that's why they've decided you work for them. At least that's what Death thinks."

I frantically started running my hands over my entire body. "Maybe I received a mark from Hell too, which means I'm still the same as the rest of the Reapers."

"Raven, no. Reapers are simply Death's employees, they don't have marks. Only Death, and now you it seems, work *directly* for Heaven."

I exploded off the couch. "Why? I haven't done anything other than my normal job. I retrieve the souls and take them wherever my portal leads. I'm a good Reaper!" I cried out.

Garrett stood and took me in his arms, my heavy tears falling onto his shoulder. I loved my job and couldn't imagine not being able to do it. He repeatedly ran his hand over my hair, trying to smooth away the anguish when suddenly, a white burst flared, creating a kaleidoscope of shimmering light behind my closed eyes.

Opening them, I found a large male angel standing in the middle of my living room. I pushed back from Garrett's hug and spun him around.

"Whoa. Who are you?" Garrett asked.

The angel smiled. "Michael." I melted at the sound of his voice. His sultry eyes rendered me speechless when he turned in my direction, his gaze locking to mine. "As you've just discovered, Raven, you've been marked by Heaven as one of our own."

Mmmm...maybe being marked by Heaven isn't so bad after all.

I stood, silent, hoping he'd continue just so I could listen to him talk. Thankfully, Garrett interrupted with a barrage of questions that needed to be answered, pulling me back on task.

"Why has she been marked? And what exactly does it mean? Will she have to leave Purgatory?"

Michael raised his hand in what I thought was a gesture to silence Garrett, but instead continued the motion, creating patterns in the air before us.

"This space is now warded; we can speak freely and no one will know I'm here."

"Okay, so why are you here? Exactly," Garrett demanded flatly.

"The gift we bestowed on Raven has finally manifested which will be a huge help in our fight against Death," Michael replied.

Garrett and I looked at one another, our eyes wide.

"Why would you be fighting against Death?" Garrett asked, addressing the elephant in the room.

Michael squinted briefly before a look of realization settled across his features. "Forgive me. I forgot I'd removed that part of your memory." He placed his sword point down on the floor and grasped the hilt. After lowering his head and muttering a few words, another bright light shone and Garrett and I were suddenly flooded with the recollection of our previous encounter with the archangel.

When his head snapped up I blushed. The feel of his lips on mine and the memory of his hands holding me against his muscular body filled my mind.

"Okay, that helps," Garrett quipped. "But again, why has Raven been marked and what gift are you talking about?"

"The gift of life, of course. Raven is now able to save someone's soul in addition to retrieving it."

"The white mist I breathed into that boy and older man. That was a gift from you?" I asked the obvious question.

"Yes, as are the dreams. They are a way for you to see the potential lives you'll be able to save."

I shook my head. "Wait, I'm confused. I've only been able to save two people, though in my dreams I've seen many more."

"That's because the human soul is still bound by free will. They can only be saved if they think of others during their last memories instead of themselves," Michael explained.

That was it; the connecting thread. Both of them *had* thought of others instead of reflecting on their own lives when their time had come. A very rare feat indeed.

"Why does that make a difference?" I asked.

"You can be their *Saving Grace*, Raven, instead of their Grim Reaper, but it's still up to them to have a heart pure enough to make it happen, that is what allows our involvement to remain concealed."

"Doesn't that go against the covenant? Heaven interfering with Death's rule," Garrett interjected.

"Death broke the covenant when he started experimenting with the phenoms. By Raven saving a soul, it keeps it out of Death's reach and lowers the number of phenoms available to him."

Yes! This was what we'd been waiting for. It was about time we got some answers as to what Death had been up to.

"What is he doing with them?" I asked.

"That, I can't tell you, I'm sorry," Michael replied.

Dammit. "Why? Technically, I'm working for you now, so why can't you tell me the truth?"

Michael stepped in my direction and I quivered. I couldn't stop my body from reacting to this man.

"Because, Raven. We don't know."

"Then how are we supposed to know what to do? How can we help if we don't know what's going on?" Garrett asked.

"Continue to do as you always have. Perform your jobs."

Michael reached for my hands. "Raven, utilize your dreams and save as many souls as possible. That alone will benefit our cause."

"What am I supposed to tell him about her mark?" Garrett interrupted. "He sent me here to find out more the instant he saw it on her tonight."

"Tell him you have no idea why she received our mark, and if he wants to question it, he can come ask us himself." Michael's tone indicated that that wouldn't be a very pleasant meeting.

"Will you leave us with our memories, this time?" I asked.

"Yes. Your gift is fully developed, and an understanding of your dreams is important to the task." Michael pulled me towards him. "And, there's something else I'd like you to remember."

Michael lifted me off the ground, and I closed my eyes. His thick arms surrounded me as his lips fell on mine. He seemed ravenous, as if starving, and I was his first meal in days. I wound my hands through his hair, just as before, and pressed myself against his hard chest. Too soon, he pulled away but kept me pinned to his body.

"Once this is over, you truly will belong to me."

I stood silent, tongue tied. The girl buried deep inside me declared, *"I was hoping you'd say that,"* but the woman and Reaper I was, forced herself to stop and think. Emotions I hadn't felt since being human flowed through me. It was like I was made to be this man's mate, but how could that be? Death created me, not Heaven, but with words like *destiny* and *cosmic intervention* steamrolling through my head while the mark throbbed behind my ear, I decided to just go with it.

We kissed again, lost in each other—completely ignoring Garrett. *Damn. Who knew angels could be this hot?*

23

It had been two weeks since Michael disappeared from my apartment. I was left wanting and frustrated, which was seriously messing with my head. I wasn't the type of girl who fell madly in love with the first guy to show interest, but Michael had a way of making me feel as if I did, in fact, already belong to him. The feel of his hands on me was seared into my brain, making it hard to focus on my daily activities.

Garrett and I did follow his directions and continued doing our jobs. Holli and I were still sent on gathering missions even though I'd saved the lives of nineteen more people. Apparently it was going to take a lot more than that to make a difference in our battle. My normal retrievals were becoming interesting, though. I continued to visit Heaven more frequently than Hell, but I couldn't determine whether it was

Michael's doing or not, since I hadn't seen nor heard from him since that oh-so-wonderful day. What was really interesting though, was when Garrett had returned to Death's castle to deliver Michael's message, he reached his chamber and found a note left on his desk, stating that Death would be gone until further notice.

"This is bullshit! All this...*'stay quiet, you're important, all will be revealed'* crap. Why can't he just tell us what's going on for Christ's sake."

Garrett eyeballed me with a raised brow. "Maybe that's exactly why they can't tell us. Perhaps what Death has been up to is affecting Heaven far more than we realize."

I popped the tops off the two beers I'd grabbed from my fridge. I'd been spending a lot more money at the liquor store lately, since we couldn't exactly talk about this stuff at the bar. Too many ears.

"Maybe. But honestly, Garrett. What do you think he's been doing that has Heaven in such an uproar?"

"I'm not sure. I just know that I wish you weren't a part of it. I hate that you are now destined to play some big role in the upcoming apocalypse."

"Excuse me? Who said anything about an apocalypse?"

"Well, what do you think will happen when Death goes up against the angels of Heaven. I'm pretty sure Hell will become involved and then BAM...apocalypse."

I laughed at his delivery, then crumbled at the validity of his statement. Things certainly were shaping up to become some sort of epic showdown.

"Have you seen or talked to Death recently?" I asked.

"No. How about you? Have you gotten any more info from Holli?"

"I asked her what they had been up to, but she said she hadn't seen much of him lately either. Which is really weird, considering how into each other they were."

"Everything about this is weird."

"I agree." The room went silent as I internally debated what Holli suggested in her fit of anger. Maybe if we simply stopped gathering the phenoms all together, we could solve the problem at its source. I'd just have to figure out a way to do that and keep both our heads in the process. Suddenly, inspiration struck. "Garrett, has a Reaper ever chosen *not* to return to Purgatory after a retrieval?"

"I don't think so, why?"

"Just curious." I shrugged my shoulders.

Garrett's intense stare had me concerned; I worried he'd pressure me for answers—answers I didn't have. Thankfully, he didn't. Probably because down deep, he really didn't want to know.

I hovered above the Sears Tower in Chicago, looking at the cloud of phenoms swarming below me. "What are you waiting for, Raven?" Holli called, her sword poised and ready. I, however, wasn't in such a hurry. I'd spent the past week thinking about my plan. If Holli and I refused to gather the phenoms, we'd most likely have to hide topside to avoid Death's wrath. I wasn't sure it would work, but if it did, I needed to make sure our hiding place would be somewhere we'd both enjoy spending our time...possibly eternity.

A chill shimmied up my spine at the thought. I wasn't ready to leave my home.

"Sorry, just thinking." I flung my ribbons in the direction of the phenoms.

Holli raised an eyebrow and lifted her sword. "Whatcha thinking about?"

I wasn't sure I could trust her with my entire plan, but I could test the waters. "Just about the overwhelming amount of phenoms and what would happen if we stopped gathering them, like you suggested before."

She shook her head. "Oh. Well, I was mad at the time; anyway, I don't think it would be good if we stopped. Wouldn't the phenoms turn into ghosts and terrorize the living?"

Dammit. She had a point.

It was why Death had given us these perks to begin with, so we could keep Earth ghost free. And, as much as I wanted to stop him from whatever he was doing, I couldn't willingly cause a problem for others. It wasn't in my nature.

"Yes, you're right. Just forget it."

Holli smiled, innocently as usual, and moved onto the next cloud a few buildings away. I headed back to the portal after snagging my fill and stepped through without waiting.

As the phenoms were sucked from my ribbons and into the blackened sky, tears spilled down my cheeks. Angry tears. Tears born of frustration. I hated trudging along, doing nothing more than going through the motions. I needed answers.

I prepared to take flight just when Holli stepped through the portal behind me.

"Got 'em all," she declared.

I nodded and pushed off the ground. "See ya later, Holli."

"Hey, what's wrong? Why are you crying?"

Ugh! I did not want to get into this with her. She could be part of the problem for all we knew, but I was so angry I couldn't hold my tongue.

"I'm upset, Holli. I want to know what Death's been up to, and why all these phenoms are popping up out of the blue." I gestured to the sky. "Something's wrong, and no one around here seems to notice or give two shits that something's up."

Holli lowered her head, her shoulders curling inward. "Sorry, Raven. I don't know what to say. Gathering the phenoms is my only job, that's all I know." Tears started to shine in her eyes.

"Holli, I'm not mad at you. I don't think it's your fault, but whatever is happening isn't normal."

She raised her head, her lips quivering. "I'd offer to ask Death what's going on for you, but I haven't seen him in weeks." She fell to her knees and buried her face in her hands.

I lowered myself back to the ground and crouched in front of her. "Holli, I'm sorry. I didn't mean to upset you."

She lifted her head, her sad eyes shining in my face. "It's not you. Things were so wonderful when I arrived, but now, it's like he's forgot all about me. The only thing I get to do is fly to the portal fields for our gathering missions and return to the castle once I'm done. I'm just so lonely."

"Why don't you come hang out with me for a while? If Death's not around, he shouldn't notice if you're gone."

She wiped away her tears and smiled shyly. "I actually tried to come see you the other day, but when I veered from my usual flight path, I felt a pop and suddenly appeared back in my room." She shrugged. "I guess I truly can't do anything without his permission."

"Wow. I'm so sorry."

"It's okay, there's nothing you can do about it."

I was now more determined than ever to prove her wrong.

24

I hovered in the netherworld, poised at St. Mary's—the very hospital I'd worked at when I was alive. I'd only returned here a few times since becoming a Reaper, but every time I did, the emotions rode me hard.

The teenage girl on the gurney was headed into surgery. I'd seen her face in my dream last night, and hoped I'd be able to save her today. Just as Dr. Taylor started to operate I felt a chill in the air. I looked over my shoulder and saw Death emerging from the shadows.

"Hello, Raven."

My muscles tensed. "Sir."

The sudden break in his recent absence didn't bode well for me. Silence hung in the air as we watched my friend perform his skillful work.

"This is where I first laid eyes on you. Did you know that?"

"No, Sir. I didn't."

"This hospital had just experienced a large influx of patients after a bus accident. I'd been watching my Reapers work the scene through my gazing pool when you entered the room."

Crazy. I had never given much thought as to how or why Death had chosen me all those years ago.

"Why did you choose me? I couldn't have been the only nurse you'd seen here that day."

"Of course not, but you were the only one who'd already been touched by death."

My head snapped in his direction. "What do you mean?"

"Your medical condition, Raven. Every time you experienced an episode, a little part of you died."

I stared at him, gauging the validity of his statement. I let my mind wander back through every episode I'd ever had. I thought about each time that I'd lowered my head, closed my eyes, and trained my breathing, and could now recall seeing a white light just before my vision had cleared and the episode had passed. I could only assume it was in those moments that a small piece of me had faded away.

"It's a very rare thing, Raven. Dying a little without becoming an actual white-lighter. It was that connection that continued to draw me back to you. I watched you every day for months, getting a feel for the kind-hearted person you were. Then, you had your final episode and joined me."

I didn't know what to say. Since becoming a Reaper, I prided myself on being strong, someone people feared and respected, yet here was Death telling me he'd chosen me because we had a connection, and that I was a kind-hearted person. I felt exposed, vulnerable, and I didn't like it.

"Thank you for telling me, I had no idea," I replied somberly. "What was Holli's condition? I can only assume she had also been touched by death."

"Yes. Holli is the same as you in that way, though plagued by a different ailment." He waved his hand. "Nothing worth talking about. Now let's see...it looks like it's time for you to get back to work."

I turned back to the operating table to see the young girl take her final breath, and froze.

Oh shit! If Death saw me save her, everything would be ruined.

Please think of yourself, please think of yourself.

I stood there, sick to my stomach, hoping this girl would die so I could keep my secret. I blinked back the tears that threatened to spill. I was usually good at hiding my emotions, but right now, I was leveled.

The girl's soul rose from her body and looked in my direction.

I breathed a sigh of relief while Death simply smiled and disappeared.

I flared my wings and I beamed at the girl. "Please don't fear me. I'm only here to help you find peace."

She nodded and took my hand.

Suddenly, something flickered in the air, catching my eye. I squinted, trying to make it out, while my inner light continued to build.

I laughed.

A small white feather drifted before me, landing softly at my feet.

"Thanks for the assist," I called out, after watching the girl walk through the gates and evaporate into thin air.

"You're very welcome."

I spun in the direction of the deep voice and smiled. Michael was gliding down from above me with nothing on but a pair of low slung jeans. Tattoos marred his glistening bronze skin, and his dark, caramel-streaked hair was a sexy mess. He was glorious.

"You needn't worry about Death discovering your gift. We are constantly monitoring the situation and will step in whenever necessary," he explained.

I stood silent, processing his words. *I should be happy that he has my back, right? Right.* So why did the grateful words I'd planned to say catch in my throat? "If you've been monitoring me, why haven't I seen you before now? Are you avoiding me? Have our encounters meant nothing to you?"

Gag. I could not believe I'd just said that, but I couldn't help the way I felt. I sounded like a desperate girlfriend and that pissed me off. How was it possible I'd become so insecure after only two kisses? "Never mind. I'm outta here." I turned to storm off, hoping my anger would trigger my inner light so I could hasten my escape.

"Please wait."

I froze. I wasn't sure if it was his gentle tone, or the fact that I so desperately wanted to hear what he had to say, or even worse, if he had some sort of control over me now that I worked for Heaven—but stop and wait is exactly what I did.

He pressed into my wings and slid his hands down my sides, bringing them to rest on my hips. He pulled me into him; his belt buckle hitting my lower back.

"I'm sorry you've felt avoided. That was not my intention. I simply thought it would be easier for us to stay apart until this is over and we no longer have to hide our connection."

"What connection? I don't even know what this is."

He spun me around, moving his hands up to cup my face.

"I've already told you, Raven, when this is over, you will belong to me."

"You make it sound as if I don't have a choice."

"Would you choose otherwise?"

"I'm not sure. But aren't we all about free will? Heaven, Death, the Reapers? We're all so concerned about the choice that has to be made at the end of our lives, yet you make it sound as if I won't be afforded the same."

He studied me with an intensity that almost burned, his gaze coming to rest on my lips. "I can't remove your mark, but I will let you choose when the time comes. Is that what you want to hear?"

Yes. No. "Thank you."

"You're welcome. And as for what *this* is..." His lips met mine, and I was transported again, Heaven merely a pit stop on my trip towards ecstasy.

25

"Why are you so giddy?" Garrett asked.

I smiled and set my drink back on the bar. "I'm not giddy. Just happy we decided to take a break from the *fight*."

He eyeballed me, gauging my response. "BS, you're hiding something."

I laughed out loud. "Fine. During one of my retrievals today, Death paid me a visit."

His eyes widened. "And *that's* put a smile on your face?" he interrupted.

"No...the trip I took to Heaven afterwards did." I squirmed in my chair.

"Ah ha. So how is the archangel?"

"Shhhh...shut up. Someone could overhear." I gawked around the bar, my eyes darting to each Reaper's face, looking for signs as to whether they'd overheard us or not. It wasn't like the words 'Heaven' or 'Hell' were out of place in our conversations, but I was pretty sure the words, 'angels', 'archangel', or 'Michael', would perk a few ears. I was relieved when the Reapers continued to lift their drinks and shift on their stools, oblivious.

"Not here, okay?" I suggested.

"Sure, sure. You're right." He nodded and turned his attention back to his drink. We sat quietly, sipping from our glasses—his filled with whiskey, mine with Amaretto. When Garrett had suggested we come here to blow off some steam, I thought it had been a good idea. Now...not so much.

"So, what did Death want, anyway?" Garrett's question broke the silence.

"Oddly enough he didn't open up and tell me his deepest darkest secrets," I teased, rolling my eyes. "Honestly, the entire thing was so strange. He reminisced about the first time he saw me, almost to the point of sounding nostalgic. I thought he was there to check up on me and ask about my mark, but he didn't."

"Did he say where he's been?" Garrett asked.

"No. I wanted to ask but doubted he would be very forthcoming."

Garrett shrugged, and we fell back into an uncomfortable silence.

Death's appearance had certainly unnerved me, as did my time with Michael afterwards, because for the second time in my life, it appeared I was headed in a completely different direction. I couldn't stop thinking about what Michael said about me belonging to him when this was over. While the thought of being with him certainly put a smile on my face, it was the opposing idea of losing my job and leaving Garrett that truly pulled at my heart.

Lost in thought, I'd missed the commotion on the far side of the bar. I looked up and focused, then tore from my seat.

Holli was standing in the doorway, frantically looking from side to side.

"Holli, what's happened?"

"Oh thank goodness you're here." She grabbed my arms. "I'm not sure what's going on, but I think it's bad." Panic marred her sweet features, and her eyes welled with tears.

Murmurs rose and the crowd started to churn, signaling we were out of time. A quick glance back at Garrett showed he'd already left his perch and was making his way towards us.

I nodded to him and pushed Holli out the door. I grabbed her hand, shot into the sky, and headed for my apartment—something that should have been impossible due to Death's restrictions.

We flew straight to my window and I quickly ushered her into the bedroom.

"Okay. Tell me what's happened. How are you even here right now?"

She sat down on the bed and lowered her head. After taking a couple of deep breaths she began. "I was standing on my balcony, alone as usual, when suddenly a loud '*POP'* rang out. I fell forward, pushing past Death's boundary, and into the sky. When I righted myself in the air, I noticed I was beyond my previous limit and decided to see how far I could go." She paused and raised her eyes to mine. "It seems I can go where ever I want now." There was a cold edge to her words.

"That's great! Doesn't it mean Death's lifted his magic?"

"No, that's just it. I don't think so. I think something's happened to him."

"What do you mean?"

"Death would never willingly remove the magic he's placed on me, but somehow it's gone. Burst, like a bubble, and I have a bad feeling that can only mean something bad has happened to him, or..." she started to cry full-on.

"Or what, Holli?"

"Or he's decided to leave me here and remain topside forever."

Holy shit! How had I forgotten about this piece of information? I now recalled being so sure that Death's visits topside to see Holli were a big part of this puzzle, but with everything that had happened—Garrett's disappearance, Michael's involvement, my gift manifesting—it had completely slipped my mind.

I started to pace. *How does this all fit together? What the hell are we missing?*

A knock on my front door announced Garrett's arrival. *Thank God!* I knew he'd come straight here to make sure we were okay, and his timing couldn't have been better. I motioned Holli towards the living room and yanked open the door, quickly pulling him inside. "We have a problem."

"Um...yeah, I figured that out when Holli crashed the party! What the hell is going on, how was she able to leave the castle?"

I waved my hands in the air, interrupting him with a plea for silence. I needed to think. I was on the verge of uncovering something; I could feel it.

It took a few more monotonous trips back-and-forth across my living room, but finally, my head snapped up. "I think I know why Death visited me during my retrieval today and why his magic isn't working here at the moment."

"Why?" Garrett asked.

"I think he hitched a ride with that girl's soul to sneak into Heaven."

Garrett flinched. "Why would he need to sneak into

Heaven? He can visit whenever he wants."

"Yes. He can move between Heaven and Hell, materializing and making his presence known, but what if he didn't want them to know he was there? What if he wanted to spy on them?"

Holli sat quietly, looking between the two of us. I wasn't sure if we should continue our conversation in front of her or not, but relaxed a little when she piped up."You could be right, Raven. Death can't see into Heaven or Hell using his gazing pool, so if he needs something from either place, he'd actually have go there in person."

"How do you know that?" Garrett asked.

"The day we left Raven in the graveyard, he transported us directly to his throne room. He looked frantically into his gazing pool, trying to see into Heaven to gain insight into Raven's mark. He was furious when he was unable to do so. I think he forgot I was watching."

"There's something else," I added.

Garrett flopped down on the couch and shoved his hands through his hair.

"Holli mentioned something to me awhile back that I thought may be important, but with everything that's happened since, I forgot to bring it up."

He huffed and gestured for me to continue with an impatient swipe of his hand.

"She told me that during her training, Death visited her topside every day for months, before and after her death."

Garrett's eyes went wide. His mouth slacked while his head shook back and forth.

"What? What does that mean to you?" I demanded.

He didn't respond. His chest began rise and fall rapidly while the look in his eyes grew wild. Obviously, I'd been right to assume this was something really bad.

"Garrett, tell us, please," I pleaded.

He stood and claimed my previous path across the carpet. Again and again, he walked the length of the room, mumbling to himself, his head never ceasing its swing of denial.

"Dammit, Garrett! Stop and tell us what's wrong," I shouted.

His abrupt halt sent me crashing into his back. He spun and gripped my arms tight. "Raven! Give me a fucking minute, okay? This is important, and I need time to think it through," he said through clenched teeth.

Garrett had never cursed at me before. I nodded and moved to sit next to Holli, allowing her to grab my hand. We remained silent and watched Garrett carry on a sometimes internal, and other times external, conversation with himself. The few words that drifted through the air made no sense at all. "*Solstice. Equinox. Impossible.*" I held my tongue while he continued to rant.

After working up a sweat and downing two beers, Garrett sat down across from us, took a deep breath, and began to fill us in.

26

"What I'm about to tell you is something no other Reaper knows," Garrett began.

Holli and I nodded our heads.

"As part of the covenant, Death is only allowed to visit topside four times a year, once every season on the solstice or equinox."

Holli and I looked at one another; the weight of his statement hung heavy in the air. I dove in, asking my question first. "Then how is it that he appeared in my apartment when I died? It wasn't on a solstice or equinox."

"No, that's not what I mean. Death can materialize anywhere in Purgatory, or travel between Heaven and Hell, and visit topside when someone dies because all those places reside in the netherworld. What I'm talking about is actually walking the Earth as a fully coalesced person."

I looked at Holli again, just as she added, "But he did. Every day for at least three months *before* I died. That's when he taught me how to fight. It wasn't until I passed on that I got my wings and began training to fly."

Garrett scooted to the very edge of his seat and reached out for Holli's hands. "So you're saying, that while you were alive and still human, Death appeared to you as a normal man, in *your* world, everyday for three months before your death?"

"Yes. That's *exactly* what I'm saying. Then, once I'd died, he officially recruited me to be a Reaper and gave me my wings. I remained topside, hidden in the netherworld, while he trained me to fly. It wasn't until I'd met his approval in both areas before he actually brought me through to Purgatory," Holli explained.

I leaned back, crossing my arms. "Okay. So let me see if I got this straight. Death can materialize and move through the netherworld unimpeded, but he can only become corporeal and walk the Earth four times a year. But now, it seems he's somehow figured out a way around that, and I'm assuming by your reaction, Garrett, this is the 'very bad thing' we've been trying to figure out all this time, right?"

"Right," Garrett acknowledged.

I continued on in a rush. "Okay. But why? Why is it a bad thing if Death walks the Earth whenever he wants? Maybe it's a stupid question, but if he's allowed to do so four times a year, why does it make a difference any other time?"

A white light filled the room, cutting off Garrett's response. Michael, once again, stood in my living room, looking magnificent as always.

Holli leapt from the couch, screaming bloody murder and pulled her sword from her belt. I grabbed her arm as the weapon extended to its full length.

"Protect yourself, Raven. He's here to kill us both!" she screamed.

I looked at Michael and back at Garrett, who'd moved to the far side of the room, plastering his back against the brick of the fireplace.

"Holli, calm down. This is the Archangel Michael, and I promise you, he won't hurt us."

"Lies! Death told me of his kind. It's their mission to rid the world of any female Reapers Death creates." For the first time since meeting her, Holli actually looked scared, and it was obvious she believed what she was saying.

I tightened my grip on her arm. "Holli, you're mistaken. Listen, if that were true, how would I still be here?"

"I don't know how you've escaped their wrath, Raven, but don't be naive. Why do you think you have been the only one for so long? They've killed all the others Death attempted to create, and that's why I was taught to fight and given this weapon. So I could not only protect him, but myself as well."

I turned to Michael, desperate for a little assistance. "Michael, will you please say something?"

My palms started to sweat as Michael remained silent and stoic. *There's no way she could be right. Is there?* A quiver rippled over my lips as the question settled on the tip of my tongue.

I opened my mouth, then noticed Michael chanting under his breath as he gripped the hilt of his sword. Suddenly, another burst of light struck out, filling the room. Thankfully, this time when it cleared, Garrett and I weren't passed out on the floor. Holli, unfortunately, didn't fare so well.

"Okay. What the hell is going on?" I demanded.

"I'm sorry. There was obviously no talking her out of these false delusions. Besides, she cannot be allowed to retain all the information she's learned here tonight. Her involvement with Death makes her too much of a risk."

I started to protest, since she'd been the one to validate most of our ideas tonight. But, before I could form the words, Michael's free arm was wrapped around me, his lips pressed boldly into mine.

"I'm pleased to see you again so soon."

I smiled. "I can tell."

Garrett coughed from his position across the room.

Michael released me which left a cold distance between us. I didn't like it. And I really didn't like that I didn't like it. How could this man be affecting me so much so soon? I was already craving his touch and missing it when it was gone. I shook my head. *Questions for another time.* We had to get to the bottom of this.

"Okay, so let's talk about this," I prompted. "Did you know that Death figured out a way to travel topside whenever he pleases?" I saw no point in beating around the bush.

"Yes. But there is much more to it than either of you know."

I placed my hands on my hips. "So let's have it."

"Perhaps we should move Holli to your bed, before we begin," Michael suggested, looking down at her prone form, sprawled on the floor. "I've erased her memories of this night, and she'll remain asleep until I want her to wake."

Wow. His power was impressive. Scary impressive.

"Of course. Garrett?" I motioned for his help. We lifted her easily and carried her to my room, and minding her wings, laid her gently on the bed. Upon our return, we found Michael relaxed on the couch, his ankle crossing his knee. He gestured for me to join him.

I didn't want to be rude, but being near him made it hard to focus. "Sorry, I think I'll stand."

Michael smiled, as if he knew exactly what I was thinking.

"All right, let's begin. Though you may already know some of this story, it has many parts and begins a very long time ago, so prepare for a long tale."

Garrett settled into the chair, and I propped myself against the fireplace and nodded for Michael to begin.

"The covenant that gives Death his power has many specific rules that were laid out by both Heaven and Hell. Death's Reapers are always male, chosen automatically in accordance with the world's expanding population at the time of their human deaths. They are required to look and operate in a certain way—obeying the law of free will. This has always been the way of things and cannot be changed."

Garrett and I remained still while Michael continued to explain.

"Another less-known aspect of the covenant, however, revolves around Death's pardon from Purgatory four times a year. His reward for keeping the balance, if you will. The bargain was struck and through the melding of spirits from both Heaven and Hell, Death is allowed to walk the Earth only during those times."

"Wait. What do you mean, through the melding of spirits? And I've always wondered, why only four times a year?" Garrett asked.

"Only during these cosmological events is the feat possible. On the morning of a solstice or equinox, an angel from Heaven and a demon from Hell are sent to Death's chamber to prepare him for his pardon. A small piece of each of their souls are placed within Death, then he's transported to Earth to begin his visit. By the end of the day the soul fragments dissolve and he's transported back to Purgatory."

Whoa.

"What does he do on Earth that would make him want to visit more often? If he likes power so much, he's got plenty of it here, why would he venture to a place where restrictions are put on him, as I assume they are?" Garrett questioned.

"Actually, it's quite the opposite. It's the restrictions in Purgatory we think Death is trying to escape."

What the heck? I was so confused, but luckily Michael continued to shed light on the situation.

"Death is no longer the same as you or Raven, he cannot enjoy the taste of food, or quench his thirst with a good wine. He is as dead as the phenoms of this world. That is the price he pays for the magic he wields. It's only on Earth that he's able to experience the joys of such things again. I imagine that's now the life he craves after serving as *Death* for so very long."

This was blowing my mind. I thought back to our dinner in Holli's room. Death had joined us, but I couldn't remember him partaking in any of the food or drink. "So you're telling me all of this is because he wants to quit his job?" I declared. "You've got to be joking."

"The position of Death isn't something one simply *quits,* and therein lies the problem. If Death were to remain topside for too long, Purgatory would fall and the Reapers would cease to exist; ghosts would overrun the Earth, and Heaven and Hell would battle for control."

Garrett looked straight at me. "What did I tell you? Apocalypse!"

27

After the shock wore off, Garrett continued to hammer Michael with questions. "What does any of this have to do with Raven?"

"Ah, yes. Now we come to the next part of the story."

"Great! How many parts are there? Aren't we already neck deep?" I quipped.

"As you're both aware, there are three things that can happen during a Reaper's retrieval. One: The person's soul chooses to willingly go with their Reaper, and depending on their pre-destined fate, are delivered either to Heaven or Hell, via the Reaper's portal. Two: The person's soul chooses to not go with their Reaper, and instead tries to run. This is a choice we have to let them make in order to honor free will. The runners are then stuck to their Reaper until they return to Purgatory where they become phenoms; lost souls. Three: In rare cases when a runner escapes his Reaper, they remain on Earth as a ghost. There was no way for a ghost to be brought back to Purgatory...until you, Raven."

Garrett and I exchanged a dark look as tension filled the room.

"Things changed the day Death figured out a way to create a Valkyrie," Michael stated.

"What?" I balked.

Garrett's head snapped in my direction.

"Garrett's correct. I *am* talking about you, Raven."

"What? No. There's no way I'm a *Valkyrie*. This is completely ridiculous." I frantically shook my head back and forth.

"Please listen and let me explain." Michael continued. "In Norse mythology, Valkyries were known for being female figures with the task of choosing who lived and died, then escorting the fallen soldiers to the hall of the slain. They were also sometimes accompanied by ravens. When Death felt the connection of life and death that your *female* spirit possessed, he borrowed from this ancient system and created you to do his bidding. This was done outside of the covenant, and therefore allowed him to mold you and give you perks that no other Reapers could ever have."

My jaw popped and my wings flared. I wasn't sure which words pissed me off more, "do his bidding" or "created" and "molded."

"So you're saying that as long as Death chooses a female, he can turn them into whatever kind of Reaper he wants. Giving them perks and 'molding' them to serve a specific purpose?" Garrett reiterated.

"Not exactly. As I mentioned—and I believe as Death has recently explained to Raven—it's due to her illness that she was predisposed to become a female Reaper. Not just any woman will do."

I looked at Garrett. "He's right. Death told me that he recruited me because of my ailment. That I'd been touched by death while I lived, and that's why he was able to make me a Reaper."

"Yes. And it was something neither Heaven or Hell foresaw, but a loop-hole Death took full advantage of," Michael summarized.

I pushed off the couch and with a quick pump of my wings, glided to the kitchen. I snagged a beer and walked back to the living room, hoping I hadn't bent the hinges on my refrigerator.

"Okay. So now we know I'm only here because Death created me to be his bitch. And we know he suddenly wants to live large on Earth in a permanent sort of way. But HOW does all this relate to Holli or the increase in phenoms, and why Death would need to sneak into Heaven?" I chugged the beer, not minding the loud, un-ladylike gulps I made.

After lowering the bottle, I stared at Michael, but it was Garrett who spoke up.

"I think I can help here." He turned to Michael. "You said he needs a piece of an angel's soul and that of a demon's from Hell to be able to visit Earth, right?"

Michael nodded with a quick dip of his chin.

"Most likely, that's where he's been during his absence. To Hell first, and now, to sneak into Heaven." He raised his hand to halt the slew of questions he knew were headed his way, then turned to me. "And Raven, you said that Holli's only purpose here was to help you collect the increased number of phenoms that started showing up, right?"

"Yep. That and apparently to protect Death from the hit-squad over here." I joked, gesturing at Michael.

"Okay. Then let's think back to the one thing you're forgetting to mention," he instructed.

"How the hell am I supposed to think about something I'm obviously forgetting? Cut me some slack here, Garrett, there's been a lot going on."

"Yes, a lot has been going on. Including your lovely visit with Holli to her secret castle and the Phenom Room you told me about."

Oh shit! I had completely forgotten about that.

"What is a *Phenom Room?*" Michael asked, leaning forward in his seat.

"Apparently Death created a hidden castle for him and Holli to frolic in. It exists in an alternate dimension which no one can see or sense, according to Holli." Garrett went on to relay the details from our previous conversation.

"Holli said that Death wanted a place where they wouldn't be watched and could be safe," I continued to explain. "At the time I thought he meant to keep her safe, but now, I think it's to keep his secret safe. There is a large room, with a black steel structure that Death uses to pull the phenoms inside. You already know he's been experimenting with them, right? Well, this is the place."

Michael's jaw flexed and his breathing grew heavy.

"So, here's what I think Death's really been up to," Garrett added. "Raven, you said that he visited Holli on Earth every day before her death, correct?"

"Yes."

"Okay. Well, we already know you were right about Death being responsible for the increased number of phenoms."

Michael interrupted. "Yes, and that's why we gave Raven the ability to save people, to effectively lessen his pool."

"All right, stay with me here. What if all the phenoms that float through the sky in Purgatory had a purpose?" Garrett posed.

"Wait...what? I thought once they were sucked into Purgatory the whole point was for them to NOT have a purpose. They are lost souls...stuck for eternity," I countered.

"True, but what if Death figured out a way to use them to make trips to Earth?"

My jaw hit the floor.

Garrett raised his eyebrows, and that cocky bob to his head was a tell-tale sign he thought he had it all figured out. "I think, based on the process used during his pardon, Death's formulated a way to use a massive amount of souls from Purgatory to become corporeal and visit the real world. *But*...until he's able to infuse them with the pieces of soul from Heaven and Hell, they would only sustain him for a short amount of time. That's why he created Holli. So you and she could supply him with an endless buffet of phenoms that he could test his theory on, until he could find a way to make his stay permanent."

Michael's power began to build and the air thickened. I could feel the hum of it slide across my skin and worried what the outcome would be. I didn't want to lose my memories again.

"If your hypothesis is true, it appears we're at the final stages of Death's plan. I have to return to Heaven and stop his search for the missing piece of an angel's soul." Michael stood and kissed me, barely leaving a thought in my head, and in another flash, disappeared.

28

I'd spent the night asleep on my couch; Garrett chose the floor. Holli had yet to wake up and was still sprawled across my bed. I wondered if Michael had forgotten about her? I didn't mind her being here, as a matter of fact, I was happy she was free of Death and that damn castle.

Garrett stirred, throwing off his blankets. "Morning," he said groggily.

"Hey."

"So. What do you think about last night?" he asked without hesitation.

"I'm not sure. It's so overwhelming. Truth be told, I'm having trouble wrapping my head around it all."

"Me too. Especially pre-coffee," he hinted.

I smiled and stretched, then headed straight for the coffeepot. After the brew started to gurgle, we put our conversation on hold, and I excused myself to the bathroom. I tiptoed into my shower, trying as hard as I could not to wake Holli.

As the hot water ran down my torso, I thought about everything that had been discussed and what it all meant. If Death was able to pull off his return to Earth, all the Reapers would cease to exist. That thought alone petrified me, not to mention the rest of the fallout.

As I ran my hand up my arm, working the soap into a bubbly lather, I paused when my fingers brushed across the raised mark. This confused things, of course.

I'd made it a point to let Michael know that I wanted a choice in what happened when all of this was over, but now I worried my choice would be tainted with the knowledge that it may be the only way to save my ass. The thought disgusted me. I wasn't one to flinch at the slightest hurdle or look for an easy way out, but I didn't want to die either.

I closed my eyes. It was all too much to think about.

I finished my shower, trying my damnedest to relax. It wasn't until I stepped into the foggy air swirling throughout the bathroom, did I notice voices coming from the other room.

I wrapped myself in a towel and huddled against the door. Garrett and Holli were laughing and flirting, hard core.

"I would love to get to know you better, Holli. You're beautiful, and seem really great!" Garrett said, sounding like he was twelve.

"Thanks, Garrett. So are you, I mean, so do you," she giggled. "I would like that very much."

Their conversation stalled, and I took the opportunity to open the door. Holli released Garrett's hand and smiled up at me.

"Hey! You're awake," I said, not wanting to embarrass her.

"Yes. I didn't know where I was at first, but Garrett heard me and came to help settle my nerves.

I bet. I chuckled internally.

"Well good. I'm glad he was here to help. I can only imagine how disconcerting it would be to wake up somewhere new after being kept under lock and key for so long."

"Yes." Her head sank.

"I'm sorry, Holli. I didn't mean to be insensitive."

"No, no. You're not. It's just that I'm still worried about Death and don't know what to do about any of this."

I had to remind myself that she no longer knew what we knew. I couldn't tell her either because Michael was right; her relationship with Death was too big of a risk. Especially if he planned to take her with him in his quest for a *happily ever after*. His continued absence, however, did give me an idea.

"Well, since I don't have to work this weekend, and we haven't had any more gatherings lately, do you want to hang out here with me? We could go back to the castle to gather some clothes if you'd like."

"You'd let me stay with you?"

"Of course."

It wasn't like I was lying, but my intention was to get Holli out and about, so I could sneak in and see what was happening inside the castle. The real one and the alternate version.

Holli sat on the edge of my bed, contemplating, when Garrett spoke up.

"That sounds like a great idea. And to kick off the weekend, I'd love it if you'd join me for dinner tonight."

Yes. While I didn't doubt his blossoming crush for Holli, I also knew that he was probably very aware of my plan, and this was his way of helping.

Holli dipped her head and a sweet-as-pie smile spread across her face.

Hmmm. Maybe Death and Holli's relationship wasn't as solid as I thought. After all the lying and now with his disappearing act, maybe Holli was ready to move on, given the chance. On the other hand, maybe it was just Garrett's charm that had her beaming and rosy-cheeked.

"So, how about it?" Garrett asked again. "Would you like to join me at *Digger's* for dinner? I promise I won't let anything happen to you."

He was good for it, too. No one messed with Garrett.

Holli stole a quick glance in my direction, then stood and extended her hand. "Thank you, I'd be happy to accept."

Garrett shook her hand. I tried hard not to laugh out loud at the formality and oddness of the exchange, but I couldn't help myself. A giggle burst forth and they both frowned at me.

"I'm sorry. It's just that you're both so damn cute."

Garrett lifted a brow dramatically. "I'm not cute...I'm dangerous."

"Right," I teased, our laughter filling the air.

Once the plans were set, Holli and I flew to the castle to get her ready for her date, while Garrett agreed to meet us back at my apartment at seven o'clock.

It was twenty till and we were still in the process of changing outfits and messing with hair.

"Holli, you look beautiful. Stop fussing."

She had on a simple black dress, cut low to make the most of her cleavage. The two tiny braids in her platinum hair draped around the sides and were secured with a garnet pendant in the back. She looked like a beautiful gothic princess—dark makeup and all.

"Are you sure you don't like the red dress better?"

"I'm sure. You look stunning and Garrett's sure to think so too."

That elicited a wide smile and a cute preen from her in the mirror.

"It's time to go," I announced.

"Okay. I'm ready."

I quickly glanced at the section of the wall where her portal was located. I could only hope my touch would open it once I returned.

29

Garrett was waiting outside my door, dressed to impress. Not in a suit and tie, but in dark fitted jeans and an ice-blue button down that hugged all his muscles just right. He looked fantastic, and Holli noticed.

Their gazes met, and it was as if time stood still. I watched, a stranger outside their bubble, while they stood staring, wide eyed. I stifled a laugh and pushed past him to unlock the front door. I spun to face the couple and couldn't deny they were stunning together.

"Okay, you two, get going or you'll miss your reservation."

"Of course, you're right," Holli replied smoothly, giving her head a little shake.

Garrett tilted his head and squinted in my direction. "Yes." He leaned in, brushing a quick peck to my cheek and whispered, "*Digger's* doesn't take reservations."

I returned the sentiment and said, "Have fun," in a loud voice, then added, "I know," under my breath.

I didn't want to waste anymore time entertaining or soothing the lovebird's nerves. I had a castle to invade and needed to get a move on.

They sauntered off, and I walked inside, re-locking the door behind me. I headed straight to the bedroom, pulled on my newest leathers, and strapped on my weapons. I had no idea what I'd face if I was actually able to penetrate the castle, so I had to make sure I was going in prepared. I grabbed my knife and guns, and for the first time, wished I had a sword like Holli's.

I smiled and thought about how far we'd come.

I'd hated Holli when she'd arrived, and now, her innocence and fierce determination was something I admired. I guess Garrett was right; having another best friend wasn't so bad after all.

I flew out my window and directly to Holli's balcony. I assumed if the magic that kept her in was no more, it shouldn't be able to keep me out either.

I touched down with a slight wobble, schooling my steps in case my assumptions were wrong. It would be just my luck to walk into a wall of energy that put me on my ass, or worse, killed me. Luckily, I sauntered straight into her room and crossed directly to the tapestry.

I pulled out my knife, ready to strike, and pulled back the rug. The wall was solid gray block, but showed no ripples, and no portal.

Dammit.

I wondered if Death removed Holli's access completely now that his plan was nearing its end, or if the access point simply disappeared whenever its mistress wasn't in the room?

Or possibly...

I started around the room, my hand skimming the surface as I went. Magic was just that, *magic*—tricky, sly, and wonderful. Maybe the door had simply relocated as a result of its paranormal properties.

I moved more tapestries, pieces of art, tables and chairs, all out of the way, so I could cover every square inch of the walls. I ran my hands up and down, smoothly at first, then tapping and knocking on the cold stone, praying for a hint as to the portal's location. Unfortunately, I found nothing. The walls were just walls and my mission had quickly turned into a complete waste of time.

I sheathed my knife and took a quick breath. I stood with my hands on my hips, looking for something—anything that I could have possibly missed. My gaze landed on the wooden door that led from her room, and I smiled.

I rushed into the hallway, looking left and right. It was narrow, and thankfully, empty. I followed my gut and turned left. The space was too tight for me to fly, so I tiptoed along the space, keeping my wings tucked in.

I had no details to recall from my visit here before, since Death had transported us directly into the hallway. However, when you took into consideration that Holli's room was in a tower, it only stood to reason that you'd start to feel a decline eventually, or so you'd think.

I walked on and on, relieved I hadn't run into anyone and been discovered, but annoyed I was getting absolutely nowhere. There hadn't been any other doors or passages, and I couldn't tell whether I was heading up or down. I told myself, *twenty more steps then I'm turning back.*

It only took thirteen.

A door appeared in front of me, and in front of it, lay an enormous beast. I'd never seen anything like it in all my life—human or Reaper. It resembled a horse, but with massive claws and strips of leathery skin that spiked and twisted away from its body. It was the size of a damn elephant and filled the entire corridor. I could only assume it was there to stop anyone from entering, or in my case, exiting.

I started to reach for my knife but stopped when the beast blew out a massive breath—I almost expected it to breathe fire, burning me to a crisp, but instead we just locked eyes, gauging each other. Lightning fast, I processed the scene; a quick glance at it claws, another at its thick hide and flaring nostrils. Then, it lunged.

I ran as fast as I could, its breath ruffling my feathers with each massive exhale down my back. The long corridor seemed to magically stretch in front of me, prolonging my torture and increasing my fear. I had to reach Holli's door before this thing took a bite out of my ass.

I couldn't imagine that Death had a *guard* just for Holli, so in the chaos of fleeing for my life, I contemplated if I could have missed the entrance to his alternate castle after all.

I chanced a glance back. *Fuck!* It was gaining, and I didn't think I was going to make it. Out of options, I reached for a dagger and struck out behind me. I made contact and yelled when an ice-cold pain shot through my blade and into my hand.

My wings started to catch in the air currents my running was creating, carrying me back and up, right into the beast's mouth. I pulled them tight to my back and kept pushing forward. Just around the curve I saw Holli's door.

I burst through it, flinging myself inside. I skidded to a stop halfway across the floor. Shuffling backwards, I spun around to face the beast. Its muzzle was pushed through the door, exhaling puffs of white smoke from its nostrils.

I moved back another couple inches and regretted it immediately. The beast started to fade in and out, shifting from real to shadow right before my eyes. I prepared to throw myself up and over the balcony but never got the chance. The shadow-beast phased through the door and into the room, then reformed, solid again and ready to finish what it started. It blew out a stream of frigid air that filled the room. Tiny frozen particles drifted to my skin, hardening the second they touched me.

I was flat on my ass, encased in ice, yet fully aware. *Well, shit.*

All I could do was wait for my demise. Oddly enough, the shadow-beast turned and strolled away, apparently satisfied he'd done his job. However, I quickly realized I wasn't out of the woods. I was immobilized, stuck here until Death found me. It was brilliant, really; a guardian that could freeze anyone in place, leaving them to await their punishment...now that was true torture.

I tried to move, shifting my shoulders in an attempt to flare my wings and burst free.

Nothing. Not even an inch.

I stared through the granulated layer and took in the room through my distorted view. Maybe if there was a sturdy piece of furniture nearby, I could rock myself in its direction and use it to shatter my glacial prison.

Again, no such luck.

I was in the middle of the room with nothing close enough to work. Resolved to the situation, I simply shut my eyes.

Being frozen didn't feel anything like I'd expect. It hurt at first, like needles penetrating deep into your skin, but I think the magic which laced the beast's cold numbed everything so fast, it preserved your body before it had a chance to recognize the pain.

I had no idea how much time had passed, when I heard a faint *tink, tink, tink.*

I opened my eyes, fighting against the tiny crystals stuck to my lashes, to find Holli tapping a nail on the ice surrounding my face.

"I see you met Svell," Holli stated.

I rolled my eyes, seeing as they were the only things I could move. Holli smiled and took two steps back.

She took a deep breath and flung out her wings in a violent snap. Her feathers turned to sharp, metal blades, ending in points that could pierce a man clean through.

My mind reeled. Another perk?

Obviously.

She walked towards me and said, "Stay very still."

Ha! As if I could go anywhere.

She brought the tips of her deadly wings down on each side of the ice dome, shattering it with one strike.

I shook off the chilly debris. "Thanks."

"You're welcome."

"Anything you want to tell me?" I asked, hoping she'd elaborate on her and *Svell's* powers.

"Yes." Her cheeks started to redden. She clapped her wings together, returning them to their softened state, then said, "Garrett is amazing!"

It wasn't the information I was looking for, but it did give me the opportunity to cover my ass.

"Great! That's what I was hoping to hear. I came here to wait for you, to see how your date went. Needless to say, my arrival wasn't met with the warmest welcome."

Holli giggled. "Yeah, Svell was a gift from Death. He protects me, and my space whenever I'm not here. Sorry about that."

She opened the door, and whistled loudly.

Oh shit!

Svell came bounding around the corner in a matter of seconds. Panic rose, and I edged closer to the balcony. *Fuck this.* There was no way I was sticking around to let this ice-beast freeze me again.

The beast phased to shadow, entering the room fully, then shifted back. "Svell, this is Raven. She's my friend. No more freezing her, okay? And she can come visit me whenever she wants."

The beast huffed a hard breath, but nudged its head into Holli's shoulder. "See. He's just a big baby!" Svell nipped at the tip of her feathers and sneezed out an icy plume. Holli laughed.

I couldn't help but smile at the interaction, however, it was the fact that Holli had just given me access to her room whenever I needed it, that warmed me thoroughly.

I shook my head as my heart grew heavy. *I'm a horrible friend.*

I spent the next few hours trying to make up for using her kindness to my advantage, by listening to her discuss her feelings and thoughts about Garrett and Death.

She was definitely torn as to what she should do, but as much as I wanted to help, I couldn't seem to come up with anything constructive to offer. "I'm probably not the best person to ask, Holli. I mean, while Death has been okay as a boss, he does tend to rub people the wrong way. So honestly, I just can't wrap my head around what it is you see in him. Garrett on the other hand, has been my best friend for eons. He's smart, funny, caring and definitely not bad to look at, so yeah...he'd always be my choice."

Holli sat, nibbling on her bottom lip. "Well, I can't explain how different Death has been with me than apparently he's been with all of you, but he's treated me with nothing but kindness, and personally, I can't understand why you *don't* find him attractive." She smiled. "He's gorgeous. Blonde hair, broad shoulders, and eyes the color of a Caribbean sea." She fanned herself. "The day he appeared outside my doctor's office, I thought he'd stepped straight out of my dreams."

What the fuck? Death blonde and gorgeous? *Um. NO!* I had to talk to Garrett, but I think I just figured out how Death convinced Holli to become his lover—he cast an illusion and literally became the man of her dreams. I shook my head and tried to focus while Holli continued to make her comparisons.

"But I can totally see what you mean about Garrett. He is gorgeous, and sweet, and funny, and really seems to want to get to know me. I really like him." She flopped down on her bed, her head hanging over the end. "I don't know what to do. Things with Death started out great, but it's obvious he has other plans that don't include me now." She flipped her head up, sending her platinum hair flying. "Do you think Death will punish me if I start dating Garrett?"

It was a valid question and one I didn't think she'd like the answer to.

"Probably," I said. "But, that's if he returns and chooses to pick things up where the two of you left off. Maybe, like you said, he's moved on and therefore wouldn't care," I amended.

"Maybe."

I could only hope what I said was true. I wouldn't want Holli punished for falling for a great guy like Garrett. Besides, it was Death's fault she was even in this position; he's the one who left her behind so he could plot and plan.

"Well, hey. It's getting late. I think I'll head home and get some sleep. If you'd like to come over tomorrow, feel free. I don't have any plans, and there's something I'd like to talk to you about," I offered.

"Really? That sounds great! Do you think we could go shopping? After trying on the few dresses I have, I realized I could really use some more clothes."

"Sure. We'll head to Drey's as soon as he opens. I know he'd love to meet you."

Holli beamed, obviously excited to begin her life as a fully-integrated Reaper. I tried to put all the sincerity I could behind my smile, but it was hard when all I could think about was Death returning and taking my head off for introducing her to everyone without his permission.

30

I'd lied to Holli again. I wasn't headed home to sleep, but instead to Garrett's to get the scoop.

"Did you have any problems with the other Reapers when you and Holli got to *Digger's*?"

"Not really. I mean, obviously everyone was shocked at seeing a new female Reaper who they'd never met, but they all kept their distance. I figured it was because they assumed the same rules applied to her as they do to you. Touch her and die."

"Yeah, you're probably right."

"So, what did you find out at the castle? Did you make it to the Phenom Room?"

"No. The entrance was completely gone. I searched Holli's entire room but didn't find it anywhere." I cocked my head and raised my eyebrows. "I did however meet Svell."

"Who?"

I wasn't sure if Garrett would have known about him or not. I always thought he was aware of all of Death's secrets, but obviously with recent events coming to light, that wasn't exactly the case.

"Svell. Holli's massive ice-breathing guard-horse/beast thing."

Garrett's tone grew serious. "What are you talking about?"

"Death gave Holli a shadow-beast to protect her and her space whenever she isn't there. It's like her pet or something. It roams the hallway that leads to her room from the main castle and breathes ice that can freeze you solid." I squinted, pulling my features tight. "Trust me...I know."

Garrett blew out a breath. "I can't believe this. Death actually gave Holli an ice-hellion as a pet?"

"You've heard of them?"

"Yeah. But not for a very long time. They reside in the frozen depth of Hell known as Cocytus, or in Norse mythology, Jotunheim. They haven't been seen in centuries."

"You were obviously right about Death visiting Hell already. If he was allowed to leave with the hellion, I wonder what deal he had to make to do so and how it plays into getting a piece of a demon's soul for him to use? And what's with all the Norse references? First with Death 'borrowing' their concept of the Valkyries and now with *Svell from Yotunheim*, what's up with that?"

"That's a good question," Garrett replied, then fell silent.

"Well, speaking of Svell. Holli gave me permission to visit the castle whenever I wanted without him turning me into a popsicle again. I'll try to get back in there as soon as I can to continue my search for the entrance. It has to still be there somewhere."

"Do you think Holli would tell you if you simply asked about it?"

"I don't know. Maybe. But I'd hate for her to figure out something's wrong. Michael said she couldn't know what was going on, and I for one don't want to be the one to tell her. Did you know that her wings can turn to metal blades and that she can kick some serious ass?"

Garrett smiled. "Yes, we talked about all of her perks over dinner. She, too, has an affinity for ice and can freeze a room as effectively as Svell can if she chooses to."

"Wow. Three perks. That's...great." I tried not to be jealous.

"Four, actually."

Fuck me.

"Her sword, the ice, her metal wings, and the ability to melt people's hearts."

I flinched back. "Why the hell would she need a perk as violent as that?"

Garrett laughed, filling his apartment with loud guffaws. *Jerk.* He was kidding, or at least meant something different than what I'd interpreted.

"Melt people's hearts, huh?" I asked, punching him in the shoulder.

"Yes, it seems so. And don't try to deny it, Raven...you like her. I know I've certainly fallen for her, hook, line, and sinker."

"That's because she's the only other woman you've been able to talk to in, oh, I don't know, forever."

"Whatever, Raven. You know I've had my fair share of women over the years. And yes, because we can only date immortals they were mostly angels—don't laugh, I know it's ironic, but Holli is different. She's innocent in all this, and that makes her sexy as hell to me."

"Well, I agree with the innocent part, and yes, she is beautiful. And fine...you're right, I do like her." I shifted on my feet. "As a matter of fact, I was thinking about asking her to move in with me. I hate the idea of her being alone in that castle. But what are we going to do if, in fact, she does end up on Death's side when this is all over?"

"I'm not sure. I guess we'll just have to hope that's not how things play out."

I nodded. *I doubt we'll be that lucky.*

After leaving Garrett's, I headed home, worn out from the day's events and still not warm after my encounter with Svell.

An ice-hellion. *Who'd have thought?*

Shaking my head at all the exhausting impossibilities I'd faced in one day, I hopped through my window and dove straight into bed.

31

I hadn't seen a light, or felt the presence of anyone in my room, so when I opened my eyes and found Michael standing over me with a sexy smile pulling at his lips, I was immediately jolted awake.

"Good morning, beautiful."

He was dressed in jeans again, and nothing else. I struggled to sit up, grasping the sheets and trying not to worry about how bad my hair probably looked.

"What are you doing here? Did you find Death? Were you able to stop him?"

Michael eased down to sit on the edge of the bed. "No. But every angel in Heaven has been notified of his plan, and all remain on high alert."

"Good." I breathed a sigh of relief. "That's good."

Michael nodded and continued to stare. I'd fallen asleep in my clothes, but the heat in his eyes left me feeling exposed nonetheless.

"So. Why exactly are you here, then?" The question came from my heart and therefore slipped right past the filters in my brain.

"I wanted to see you and make sure you were all right." He reached for my hand.

I didn't buy his excuse, as he could have easily seen whether I was *all right* or not as he done in the past by "constantly monitoring the situation." Obviously, he had another reason for being here, and by the look on his face, I had a pretty clear idea of what it was.

He started to speak, but before he could utter another word I leaned forward, entwining my fingers in his hair once more.

Our lips met with soft glances, again and again. I scooted closer until I was practically sitting in his lap. His hands roamed by back, skillfully avoiding the sensitive spots under my wings. The feel of his fingers sliding down my curves and squeezing my hips had me clinging to him as our kisses grew frenzied. He pushed me onto my back, repositioning himself until he was leaning over me, his broad shoulders filling my view.

"I want you, Raven, and I cannot wait any longer."

"Who's asking you to wait?"

"I just want to make sure you feel the same before I claim what's mine."

Dammit. Why did he have to use those words? I pushed him back and leaned up on my elbows. "Claim what's yours?"

"Yes. As I told you, you are to be mine, Raven. And though I'll give you the choice to join me in Heaven or not, that doesn't change the fact that we are meant to be."

"Oh my God! How can you talk like that? Just because I was created to be a pawn for Death, it doesn't mean I'm meant to be a pawn for Heaven, too. I don't care that you've 'blessed me' with the gift of life and intuitive dreams; that doesn't mean I'm yours to do with as you please. You can't treat people that way, whether you're an Archangel or not."

He sat back, his jaw clenched and eyes trained directly on mine. "Is that what you think? That I'm choosing to 'do with you as I please' simply because you've been marked?"

"Well, yes. That's how you're acting. That just because of this," I pointed behind my ear, "I'm now a piece of property that you can 'claim.'" I shimmied up until my back hit the headboard. "Well, let me tell you something...I'm no one's property!"

If Michael hadn't been sitting on top of the covers, I would have stomped across the room and slammed the door to emphasize my point. But, since I was effectively pinned in place, I simply crossed my arms instead. I realized that I was sending mixed signals by initiating our kiss and then putting on the breaks thirty seconds later. But damn it, there was no way I would let my libido override my self-respect.

The lazy smile that spread across his face had me squirming in my cocoon of blankets. "What?" I demanded.

"You are very attractive when you're being stern."

I leaned forward, bringing our faces within inches of each other. "You haven't begun to see me get stern." I was trying for intimidating, but instead, all I did was sabotage myself into becoming more turned on. *This is ridiculous.*

Michael smiled and grabbed me once more, stood, and lifted me straight out of bed. He cradled me in his arms and mumbled something under his breath. In a flash we appeared in Heaven, the bright light fading around us.

"Why did you bring me here? I thought you said you'd give me a choice?" I exclaimed.

"I want to show you something."

He set me on my feet and gently took my hand. We veered away from the pearly gates straight ahead and walked into what looked like a massive cloud bank off to the left. As the thick air dissipated I saw another set of gates. They were huge and stunning blue, sparkling like a tropical sea.

"I want you to see my home," Michael announced.

Oh my God!

32

As we walked through the sparkling gates, I felt like a teenager on my first date. I knew other Reapers had been here before, as Garrett had explained during his sexual proclamation where he shared with me his affinity for angels. But I, personally, had never considered that at any point in my afterlife I'd be strolling down the glistening halls and gawking at the white dolomite structures that made up the Archangel's quarters.

"This is lovely," I said, trying hard not to stutter.

"Thank you." He gestured to a large building on the right. "This is me."

The edifice had massive marble columns and a gorgeous, ornate golden door. "As in, your room is inside this building, or the entire place is yours?"

Michael simply smiled and led me inside.

The domed ceiling rivaled the Sistine Chapel with its impressive frescos—most, but not all, featuring Michael and his numerous victories. The high, arched walls and stained glass windows took me back to my time as a child when I worshipped every Sunday with my grandmother at St. Peter's.

I was awestruck. "This is absolutely breathtaking."

Michael continued to guide me through his home, from the elaborate entrance, to the more humble kitchen and living areas, and finally to the bedroom. "Um...I thought I made myself clear before." I pulled my hand from his and stopped where I stood.

"You did. I just need to show you something that resides here in my room."

He walked to the far side of his luxurious Greek-inspired, four-poster bed and picked up what looked like a small crystal from the side table. "This is an angelic seeing stone," he explained, holding it up between his fingers for me to see. "It's how I'm able to see topside and into Purgatory. I want to let you see the history of all that's been recorded within."

Before I could respond, he closed his fist around the stone and mumbled a few words under his breath. Upon opening his hand, the crystal floated into the air and began to project holographic images right before my eyes.

I gasped.

All the images were of me. From when I arrived in Purgatory to now—my smile, my tears, my laughter, my anger——all on display, shimmering directly in front of me.

"I've been watching you from the moment you became a Reaper, and I've never wanted anyone other than you." He took my hand again. "My 'claiming' you isn't about that mark behind your ear, but because Death's mistake has allowed me to make contact with you; a dream I've carried for a very long time."

I was speechless. I didn't know whether to be pissed about being spied on, or giddy that the most gorgeous and powerful angel in the world wanted only me. I shook my head and pulled out of his grasp again, then walked over to the plush chair along the far wall. I needed to sit down and process.

"I've spent an eternity waiting for the one person who could rule my heart, and that person is you, Raven. *That* is why I want you with me," Michael concluded.

I lifted my eyes to his and self-doubt invaded my thoughts. I was sure he had dated before —angels of course, but a Reaper? *Now there's a catch.* I was something new, and that *had* to be the draw.

I took a deep breath. "I'm not sure what to say. I'm flattered and definitely attracted to you, you know that. But the idea of you watching me all this time is very upsetting. It's an invasion of privacy, which if you know me as well as you should, you'd understand is a big problem for me."

Michael took a deep breath but remained in place. "I did not invade your privacy or simply sit and watch you at all hours of the day. I was tasked with monitoring the situation of a female Reaper who'd been created outside the covenant, and by doing my job, at the intervals I was instructed, I couldn't help but fall in love with you. Your strength, your selflessness, your heartfelt friendship with Garrett. All those things that I glimpsed made it clear that you were the only one for me." He crossed his arms, defiantly, making it clear he was done explaining himself.

I watched his jaw tick and knew it couldn't be easy for someone like him, a man in his position, to lay his feelings on the line.

That alone, softened my heart.

I stood and crossed the room. I placed my hands on his forearms and smiled when they unfolded and slid back to his sides. Easing closer, I ran my palms up his taut biceps and onto his muscled bronze pecs. "I will still expect to be given a choice when this is over as to whether or not I want to come live here with you. But for the time being, I'd love nothing more than to date the hottest angel in existence."

It sounded shallow, but as much as I wanted to balk at the things that should keep us apart, it was the rightness of our union that radiated from deep within my soul that pushed me forward.

I didn't have time to see Michael's sexy smile take shape, because before I could blink his lips were once again crushed to mine.

He nipped and sucked his way from my lips to my neck, then across my collarbone, the sensual feel of his mouth sending me over the edge. I reached up and secured my arms around his neck and my legs around his back, as he walked us both across the room and gently laid me across the bed. "You are so beautiful, and I'm honored you've chosen to *date* me, but you should know, I'm not into one night stands," he teased.

I smiled. "Neither am I."

33

Michael and I woke to sounds of alarm—angels yelling and loud chimes piercing the air.

I scrambled to find my clothes. "What's happening?" I asked.

"I believe Death has been found."

I froze and tried to swallow around the lump in my throat.

While stopping Death was something that had to happen, it also meant I'd be forced to make my decision long before I was ready.

I shook my head and reached for my boots. "What will happen to him?"

"It's not up to me, but I can only assume he'll be stripped of some of his power."

That made sense. The one thing that powerful men feared above all else was a loss of that power.

"Will I be able to see him?" I needed answers as to what Holli had to do with this, and explain that she was going to be moving in with me regardless of what he said. She didn't deserve to remain isolated in that damn castle with nothing but an ice-hellion as her only companion. "Hey, were you aware that Death gave Holli an ice-hellion as a pet?"

Michael spun around in a flurry, a fierce look marring his angelic features. "What did you say?"

"Um, that Death gave Holli an ice-hellion as a pet. He protects her place whenever she's gone. His name is Svell." I rolled my eyes.

Michael grabbed me by the arms and dragged me to sit on the bed. "Raven, this is important. Are you sure that Holli has an *ice-hellion*? A shadow-beast from the depths of Cocytus, and that it *belongs* to her?"

"Yes. That's what Garrett said." I shook off his hold and pushed from the bed. "What's wrong?"

"Raven, only a specific demon who's resided in the frozen level of Hell can control a ice-hellion. Holli apparently isn't who she appears to be."

I stumbled backwards. Michael caught me just before I hit the ground.

"Death found Holli topside, just like me. He recruited her because of her ailment, just like me. She can't be a demon," I breathed. "This has to be a mistake."

"I hope so, because if not, I don't think you'll be pleased to find out who your friend really is."

Well, fuck. That was ominous. "Just tell me." I collapsed the rest of the way onto the cold marble floor.

"Only the Norse Goddess of the Afterlife is considered to be half-dead and half-alive, which gives her access to Hell. Her culture views her with considerable trepidation since she can walk in both worlds, helping those in times of need, but vengeful against those who cross her. Her name is Hel, or Holle."

Oh my God. "Half-dead and half-alive, that's what allowed Death to choose her. Plus, helping those in need but vengeful against those who cross her—that sounds exactly like Holli." I closed my eyes and took a deep breath. "I can't believe this is happening."

"I'll have to test her, but if what I assume is correct, then it seems Death already has the piece of a demon's soul he requires."

I sat on the floor, my mind blank and my vision blurred. I couldn't process this new information. My head snapped up when my anger overtook my shock. "Let's go get Death. I want to see him, right now!"

Michael and I left his home and rushed toward the chaos. There was a crowd at the far end of the wide promenade. The mass of angels split when we approached, making way for Michael to pass.

"Where is he?"

The angels stuttered and mumbled, but no one offered a clear answer.

"I'll not ask again."

An angel with small wings and fiery hair stepped towards Michael, her arms crossed and her head down.

"I'm sorry, Sir. I'm afraid he was too strong for me and got away."

Dammit!

Michael stood silent, while I internally cursed. I looked back at the girl and upon closer inspection could see that her wings weren't supposed to be small, but that they had instead been damaged. "Was he able to get a piece of your soul?" I rushed to ask.

"It wasn't my soul he was after. I was just the one who found him and tried to stop him from fleeing." She took a step back and pointed past the crowd.

I squinted and in the distance saw the shape of a body lying at the base of one of the large olive trees that led to the meadow beyond. Michael pushed off with a dramatic shove of his wings and floated down to the angel within seconds. I followed suit while everyone else remained where they were.

"Is she okay?" I asked.

"No, Raven. She's dead."

34

I knelt beside the fallen angel. "How is this possible?"

Michael eased a hand down her blond hair. "Apparently Death was after more than just a piece of her soul." His eyes met mine and my heart lurched. "He took the entire thing, and in doing so, ripped out her immortality along with it."

I shivered.

I'd seen Death use his scythe to deliver the final death to an immortal before, and it wasn't something you easily forgot.

I looked back down at the angel, saddened when her wings fell from her body, becoming nothing but crystallized dust. Her skin and hair withered and within seconds coated the ground as a layer of fine sand.

A single tear flowed down my cheek.

"Why would he need her entire soul?" I breathed.

Michael stood and pulled me to him. "I can only assume that he figured the more of it he attained, the more successful his plan would be."

"Do you think he's right?"

"Considering that a small piece allows him to visit for a day, I can see how using an entire soul could extend the effect. I'd wager that with the addition of his experimental phenoms and a strong dose of magic, Death thinks he'll be able to make his stay permanent."

I let myself sink into Michael's arms. I needed his strength for what I knew was coming next.

"We have to get to Holli," Michael stated.

"I know."

He transported us straight to my apartment, since my earlier plans were to meet Holli there later this evening.

She hadn't arrived yet.

"Maybe Death got to her before she could leave the castle," I said, trembling at the thought.

"Yes, perhaps."

We started towards the bedroom window, ready to take flight, when a knock sounded from the living room.

Oh thank goodness.

I raced to the door. "Coming," I announced.

"I'm so glad you made..." My words trailed off.

Garrett practically fell through the door and into my arms, panting heavily.

"Thank God you're back," he breathed.

"What happened? Where's Holli? She was supposed to be here."

"Death took her."

Fuck!

"What do you mean, took her? As in, forcibly?" I asked.

"Yes. I saw her coming out of Drey's, but before I could reached her, Death appeared and they started arguing. She tried to fly off, but he grabbed one of her wings and she cried out. When he removed his hand there was a black smear on her white feathers and it appeared she could no longer fly. Then he grabbed her wrist and they disappeared."

My shoulders slumped, and I took a deep breath. "I was supposed to take her to Drey's today. She must have thought I'd stood her up." I flopped down onto the couch. "We might as well regroup here, and you might want to take a seat—we have a lot to tell you."

"Oh great. More good news," Garrett quipped.

Michael and I enlightened Garrett with all that we'd discovered.

"So if Holli is really the demon goddess Hel, Death already has everything he needs to complete his plan." Garrett's hair was a tattered mess from all the passes he'd made through it with his fingers.

"Yes. That's why we were headed back to intercept Holli. First to see if she is in fact Hel, and whether she's known it all along. Or if her life here has just been another illusion Death cast on her, like the one that made him appear blonde and irresistible."

"You did not tell me about any such illusion," Michael interrupted.

"I'm sorry, it simply slipped my mind," I replied. "When Holli and I were discussing her relationships, she'd described Death as being blonde with broad shoulders and dazzling blue eyes. And that he'd seemed to have stepped right out of her dreams."

Michael eased off the arm of the couch and stood at attention with his arms crossed. "Death shouldn't have that kind of power, and I think the image he chose to project is a clue as to why he does."

"Don't tell me, another Norse God?"

Michael nodded. "Yes. I think Death may have joined forces with Loki. He is Hel's father and the only person who I could imagine that would have the kind of power and the twisted sense of mischief to devise a plan such as this."

I looked at Garrett. "At least now we know why Death's been obsessing over Norse mythology."

"Yeah. Looks like he made a deal with the Norse version

of the devil and his daughter."

"How do we stop them?" I asked, looking to Michael for guidance.

"One step at a time. We need to find Holli and see if she's been a part of the plan all along."

"I'm not sure how we're going to do that. I'm the only one who's been given permission to enter her room at the castle, but I doubt that invitation still stands now that Death is back in Purgatory."

Garrett's head snapped up. "What did you say about their alternate castle before? That it dwells in a different realm and cannot be seen by others, right?"

"Yes."

"But you also said that he uses that metal device to pull the phenoms inside, correct?"

"Yes," I repeated.

"So all we need to do is wait and watch the sky for a large vortex of phenoms being siphoned into what seems like empty space. Once we pinpoint the location of the alternate castle, Michael should be able to break through the dimensions to gain us access."

"Yes. If we can find the entrance, I can get us in." Michael reached out to take my hand.

"Good. At least we have a plan." *Now we just need to not die while executing it.*

35

We watched the sky from the roof of my apartment building—Garrett, Michael, and I—all waiting and hoping for some sort of break. I was worried about Holli, or Holle, or whoever the "Hel" she was, but was hopeful that the longer it took for Death to start the last step of his plan, the more likely it was that she hadn't been a part of it.

"How are we going to get Holli away from Death long enough to find out what she really knows?" I asked.

"Well, I think once we're in, if she uses Svell and her powers to turn us to ice-cubes, we'll pretty much know she was in on it," Garrett huffed.

I gave him the dirtiest look I could muster while he tried to wipe the smirk off his face.

"Yes. I suppose that would clear things right up, wouldn't it?" I teased back.

"I'll be able to handle Hel and her ice-hellion. But Raven, that leaves you to stop Death." Michael's confidence in me was a hell of an ego boost. Through all this chaos, I felt like I'd lost a part of myself, the part that was Raven, the badass Reaper who everyone feared. Thankfully, that part had just been fully restored.

"Don't worry about Death. I'll take care of him." I wasn't sure how, but I knew Heaven had chosen me for a reason, and with Michael and Garrett by my side, I had no doubt that we could stop him.

"Look. Right there!" Garrett exclaimed. "Do you see that?"

Far off in the distance a swirl of phenoms was amassing into a large tornado that looked to be "touching down" in the middle of the sky.

"That has to be it." I said.

"All right. Once we are close, remain behind me while I gain access. Raven, you keep Garrett out of the way until I'm able to immobilize Holli and possibly Svell if necessary, then head straight for Death. Use your ribbons to ensnare him. The perk he gave you may just be the one thing that will allow us to stop him in the end."

We all nodded at one another and took flight. Michael with

his sword aloft, looking like the fiercest warrior I'd ever seen, and me, carrying Garrett just like when we'd flown above the rooftops for fun.

When we reached the spinning vortex of phenoms, Michael paused just beside the point of the storm. There was a slight warble at the very tip, and it was precisely in that disturbed space where Michael thrust his sword.

Suddenly the sky started to tear, creating a hole into Death's castle just as we'd hoped. The phenoms poured through the opening and filled the chamber in one massive tumble. It was the perfect distraction.

Michael dove inside, and I followed, placing Garrett against the far wall closest to the door. Even though we couldn't see either of them yet, we all heard Death bellow and Holli scream.

I spun around, looking from side-to-side, pin-pointing where everyone was. I spotted Michael, in the center of the room, just below the metal structure. He had his sword poised at Holli's neck.

"Wait!" I screamed.

I knew I was supposed to leave Holli to him and focus on stopping Death, but seeing her there, with that petrified look on her face, there was no way I'd be able to focus until I knew the truth.

With one pump of my wings I flew to the center of the

storm, motioned for Michael to back off, and grabbed Holli by both arms.

"Tell me the truth! Who are you?"

"I don't know what you mean?" she sobbed. "Raven, please. Help me get out of here."

It was only then that I noticed that she was tied to a pole that rose out of the floor.

I reached for the chain that was running between her wrists and the steel rod.

"Don't. They're spelled," she said in a rush.

"That's right, they *are* spelled, which means she's not going anywhere." Death's voice boomed from behind me.

Michael and I spun around, and though it was hard to see through the thick frenzy of buzzing phenoms, I finally spotted Death creeping towards us from the right side of the room.

"There," I whispered to Michael, gesturing with a slight tilt of my chin.

"Got him."

Michael pushed off and disappeared into the cloud above me. I expected him to land behind Death any second, but when he didn't, I decided to make my move.

I threw out my ribbons and smiled a wicked smile when they attached with ease. "Seems you're plan isn't going to work after all," I taunted.

I felt a slight tug on my ribbons but held tight, even as Death leered at me.

"You think you've beaten me? ME?" His voice echoed all around me as he threw his hands into the air. My ribbons fell from him as he shifted from man to shadow and back again. Suddenly, I was the one stuck, caught within the confines of the swirling black souls that radiated out from his entire body. Apparently, Garrett's theory had been correct; Death had been absorbing all the phenoms into himself.

Dammit! Where are you, Michael?

"No! Please stop. Don't hurt her," Holli pleaded.

"Don't worry, my love. In a moment, you won't care about her at all."

I struggled and strained, flaring my wings, trying anything to break free from the phenoms.

Death approached Holli, holding out his hand. His scythe materialized out of the swirling black smoke, the deadly tip glowing blue the closer it got to her temple.

Panicked, I increased my efforts, wriggling and writhing but to no avail.

"I took your memories with the help of your father, as a way to gain access to what I needed, but also to help free you from your immortal ties, as was our deal. No longer will you be stuck in Hell, just as I will no longer be stuck serving my endless sentence here."

"What are you talking about?" Holli's tears flowed in earnest.

"I'm talking about the chance for us both to live again. Really live, Holli, on Earth. Free to enjoy life, and eventually death, as it's meant to be. Once I remove most of your soul, you'll no longer be immortal, but I'll leave you with just enough so that you can join me topside, where we can live out the remainder of our very long lives."

Holli's head shook back and forth while tears continued to flow down her cheeks. "You're crazy. And I don't understand why you're doing this or what you're even talking about."

"Just hold still, my dear, and everything will become clear."

I screamed at the top of my lungs, hoping for a boost of strength, or to simply offer a distraction and delay what was about to happen.

It wasn't me, however, who gave Holli a small reprieve.

It was Krev.

36

"What are *you* doing here?" Death demanded.

"Do you think I would miss this fairy-tale ending?" Krev's voice sounded funny, odd and layered with a strange accent.

"How did you get in here?" Death asked, seeming genuinely confused.

"The same way the archangel did. I tore a hole in space." His eerie smile sent chills up my spine.

I looked up to the ceiling to see Michael, unconscious and tied to the steel structure high above our heads. His wings were frayed and torn around the edges where a shimmering green rope cut into them.

"Who are you?" I demanded.

Krev's laugh was sinister. "Hel's father, of course."

Loki.

"That's right...I can tell by the look on your face you've got it all sorted out." A shimmer in the air revealed the God behind the mask. The image of Krev disappeared and was replaced by the Norse God of Mischief; blonde, handsome, and evil through and through.

"Wave hi to Daddy." He wiggled his fingers at Holli, who looked like she was about to pass out.

I pulled as hard as I could against the souls still holding me captive but couldn't move an inch.

"Loki. My friend. You surprised me. I had no idea you'd taken on the guise of one of my Reapers."

Death was trying his damnedest to sound at ease, but I'd been around him long enough to know when he was feeling strained. And right now...I could tell he was feeling *very* strained.

"I was just about to free your daughter's memories. Would you like to do the honors instead?" Death offered.

Loki moved towards Holli, and I couldn't breathe. I certainly didn't want to meet the Goddess Hel, but more importantly, I didn't want to lose my friend.

"Wait. Please. Why do you need to take her soul? I mean, if she can travel to Hell, why don't you just have her bring you another demon to use? Then you can take her topside with you, whole and unharmed." I wasn't really sure if what I was suggesting made any sense or helped Holli in any real way, but as long as I could keep them talking, and Death's scythe away from her, I'd say anything that popped into my head.

"Because, Raven. If I want to make sure all my hard work pays off, I can't settle for anything less than the most potent souls of both Heaven and Hell. It's the only way to make my visit permanent, or at least until I die a natural death at the end of my very long life on Earth."

Panicked by his words "the most potent souls" I stole a quick glance at Michael and prayed Death wasn't planning on reaping his soul as well. *Keep him talking.*

"Why would you want that? You spent your entire existence creating the Reapers and performing your job. A job, may I remind you, that is probably the most important in the world. You alone are in charge of maintaining the balance in the universe. Doesn't that satisfy you in the slightest?"

"It used to. Until I saw that in order to do my job, it was I who had to pay the highest price. The longer I served as Death, the less *I* became." The muscles in his jaw clenched, and his knuckles turned white around his scythe. "To say it's been a miserable existence would be an understatement. So, when Loki approached me with an alternative, I simply couldn't pass it up. I've served this sentence for far too long."

I took a deep breath and couldn't deny the twinge of sympathy I felt. Even with as powerful as he was, apparently, being Death came with a downside.

"I'm sorry you feel as though this position has been a punishment, but you have Holli now. Why can't you just stay here and keep things the way they are?"

I hated offering that as an alternative, but again, I was desperate and would say anything to stall them.

"Because, part of the deal is to free my daughter from the confines of her position as well," Loki interrupted. "Hel will walk the Earth again, and I for one, can't wait to see the chaos she brings with her."

Loki's triumphant laugh was interrupted when Garrett came crashing through the door with Svell hot (or cold?) on his heels.

37

Garrett dove out of the way, leaving the ice-hellion to slide directly into Loki, who yowled in pain when his entire right arm turned to ice.

"Call off your dog, Daughter," he commanded.

"Never!" Holli screamed, then nodded her head at Svell. The beast turned and blew out a massive breath of crystallized ice, freezing both Loki and Death right where they stood. The instant their connection was severed, all the phenoms fell to the floor, covering it in a layer of black fog.

Silence reigned for a split-second before Holli exclaimed, "Garrett! Thank goodness you're all right."

I pushed off the ground and flew to Michael's side, leaving the lovebirds to comfort each other. The green rope holding Michael had lost its luminosity, so I grabbed it and tugged.

It fell away easily, dropping to the ground.

I glided us back to the floor and laid him on the tile, displacing the fog with the mass of our bodies. "Michael, please wake up." I ran my hand down his cheek and placed a kiss on his lips.

Garrett and Holli joined me, standing silently off to the side. "Is he dead?" Holli asked.

Tears filled my eyes, and I shook my head. "No. He can't be." I lowered my head and prayed my words were true.

Svell came to stand next to his mistress, his frosty breath tickling the back of my neck. We all remained still, and after a few moments, were covered in a light dusting of frost.

Finally, Michael inhaled, and the chilly flakes slid from his rising chest. "Michael!" I threw myself across him.

"Raven." He coughed. "Are you all right?"

I sat up. "Yes. Yes, I'm fine. Are you okay? What happened? How did Loki get the drop on you?"

Michael shook his head, and his expression turned fierce. "Loki! I should have known. When I took to the sky, I felt a snap at my back when I got near the dome, but that's all I remember."

I reached for the rope. "He had you tied to the structure with this."

Michael grabbed the long braid that had bound him and clutched it in his fist, turning it to ash. "His poison must have been what rendered me unconscious."

"Poison? Are you sure you're all right?" I asked, trembling.

Michael reached for me, placing his hand gently on my cheek. "Yes, my love. I'm perfectly fine. It will have no long term effect on me."

Michael released me and pushed off the floor, coming to stand in front of Loki and Death. "Svell?" he asked with a knowing smile.

"Yes." I laughed.

Michael and I turned to Holli and Garrett, who stood holding hands with the ice-hellion heeling at their side. "Thank you for saving us," he said, addressing them both.

I shook my head at Garrett's wide smirk and cocky nod. I could only imagine how I'd never live down the fact that he was the one who'd saved the day.

Holli smiled at Michael. "I'm sorry I freaked out when I first met you," she said, shyly, "but in my defense, it was only because Death had told me you would kill me."

"It's all right. His lie was no doubt meant to keep you away from me, for he knew if we were to get too close, I'd be able to sense your true nature."

Holli lowered her head and sunk into Garrett's embrace. "So it's true? I'm the demon goddess Hel, and the daughter of Loki?"

"Yes," Michael replied.

"I'm sorry," Holli answered.

We all looked at one another, then I burst out laughing. "Holli, how can you be sorry for being who you are? Like the saying goes, you can't pick your family, and it's not your fault your father's an asshole. Plus, you are the sweetest person I've ever known, so I don't care who you *really* are, to me, you're simply my friend."

She smiled and wiped a tear from her cheek. "Thanks, Raven. Do you think my memories of being Hel will stay locked away?"

We all turned back to look at the ice domes encasing Loki and Death. "Yes, as long as they can't combine their magic again to reverse the effect," Michael answered.

"What do we do now?" I asked.

"I'll take them to Heaven to receive their punishment."

"You guys can punish another God?"

Michael smiled. "Power is power, Raven. It all comes from the same source. Whether you worship the Norse Gods, the Greeks, or my own, they're all different, yet one in the same."

Michael wrapped me in his arms and kissed the breath out of me. "Think about your decision while I'm gone."

The sexy angel pulled out his sword and touched the tip to each ice dome. I was awestruck when they lifted into the air, hovering inches above the floor.

His glowing light built and at the apex exploded, filling the space in a brilliant white glow.

I shielded my eyes.

When my vision cleared, I found that all the phenoms had been erased, leaving the floor completely clean.

"So, what do we do now?" Garrett asked, repeating my earlier question.

"I'm not sure. I guess wait for Michael to return with Death and see where things go from there."

"Do you think he'll actually return?" Holli asked.

"I assume he has to. Michael said that without Death in his position, all the Reapers would cease to exist, and the world would be plunged into chaos," I summarized.

A panicked look crossed Garrett's face. "Loki feeds on chaos. What if that's still part of his plan? If Death failed, I'm sure Loki would double-cross him in a second to bring about the end of the world."

I sneered. *Fuck!* "Back to the apocalypse it seems."

It didn't take much for my anger to build and my portal to open. I reached for Holli and Garrett.

We all appeared outside the sparkling gates, and I looked around, wondering which direction to head.

"Raven?"

I recognized the red-haired angel that tried to stop Death on his previous visit. "Yes. Hello. Can you tell me where Michael is?"

"He just passed through the main gates, taking the prisoners to face their judgments."

"Great. We have to get through there. Are we able to pass?"

"You can, yes, because of your mark. But they cannot." She gestured to Holli and Garrett.

"Fine. Can you take them to Michael's quarters and wait for us there?"

"Of course."

Garrett nodded and attempted a smile, while Holli rushed to give me a quick hug. "Be careful," she whispered.

"I will."

I paused, watching Garrett and Holli walk hand-in-hand into the cloud bank, then proceeded to enter the pearly gates.

The clouds were thicker here and brushed softly against my skin. I took each step with caution, worried I'd hit some barrier or sink through a hole that was meant to claim unwelcome visitors. Luckily, neither was the case.

As the fog lifted, I had to force myself to remember why I was here. The grandeur of Heaven was beyond compare and an overwhelming distraction. Cascading waterfalls, lush vegetation, sparkling buildings, and in the distance a colossal castle resting on a mountain.

I flew to the entrance and stood outside the enormous see-through door. There was no handle or seam marking a way for it to open, only a large square barrier of pure crystal at least three feet thick, blocking my way. I contemplated knocking, but instead decided to lay my palm flat against the door. The mark behind my ear warmed, and the obstruction disappeared. *Thank God.*

I rushed inside and raced to catch up to Michael.

38

I ran down the long corridor and rounded the corner, spotting Michael at the far end of the next hall.

"Michael!" I called out.

He spun around and smiled, confident yet surprised. "Have you made your decision so soon?"

I shook my head, slightly embarrassed. "Um, no. I'm sorry, that's not why I'm here. Garrett thinks Loki has an ulterior plan. He feels that since Death failed, Loki will attempt to eliminate him in an effort to destroy Purgatory anyway. I came to warn you."

Michael sheathed his sword, which caused the ice domes carrying Death and Loki to gravitate back to the ground. He took two steps towards me and pulled me into a hug, nuzzling my ear.

"Thank you for your concern," he kissed my mark, sending a shiver across my skin.

I closed my eyes, and for a split second, allowed myself to enjoy the feel of his body against mine.

Tink, tink.

My eyes snapped open.

"Michael, look out!" I shouted.

The metal blade of Death's scythe was glowing bright blue.

The dome around him shattered, bursting in an explosion of ice. I pushed Michael to the side and flung out my ribbons, ensnaring Death before he could make a move.

Michael drew his sword and stalked to Death, who was attempting to fade to shadow.

"You will not escape again." The tip of the archangel's blade rested under Death's chin.

Michael chanted under his breath, and the air grew thick with magic.

My eyes grew wide as Death went rigid—turning as solid as a board—and floated inches into the air.

Michael moved passed him, leaving him to dangle in stasis, and let out a frustrated breath. "Loki has escaped, but Death will not go unpunished. Release him and let's go."

I drew back my ribbons and followed Michael down the hall, stopping to stare at the now empty ice dome which previously held the Norse God of Mischief.

I reached out a finger and jumped back when it shattered at my touch. "Where do you think he went?"

"I can't be sure. Home, to regroup most likely."

This is all my fault. "I'm sorry I distracted you. If I hadn't come, you wouldn't have turned your back on them."

"Don't be silly, it was only a matter of time before their powers broke through. With centuries to plan and an endless supply of magic to wield, I knew Death would have a trick or two up his sleeve. And to be honest, if you hadn't been here, I'm not sure I would have had the chance to stop Death before he turned to shadow and disappeared, or before Loki was able to complete his mission and eliminate him all together. I'm grateful for your presence."

I managed a small smile but couldn't shake off the guilt. I remained quiet as we walked further into the castle, Death floating in the air between us, guided by the tip of Michael's sword.

We continued down elaborate corridors that shimmered as if the walls were liquid. Our movements caused them to ripple and roll, fanning out in tiny waves as we passed. I was completely mesmerized.

After a few more twists and turns, we reached the main chamber.

"Wait for me here," Michael instructed. Focused again, I started to protest, but Michael smiled and shook his head. "I'm sorry, but there's no alternative. You cannot pass."

I smiled and nodded, overwhelmed by how proud I was of him and the position he held. "I'll be right here."

I paced outside the golden chamber for what felt like an hour, though it was probably no more than fifteen minutes. Finally, Michael emerged...alone.

"Where's Death?" I strained my neck to look behind him.

"After much debate, and no doubt under duress, he requested to be destroyed. The alternative he was offered was clearly not something he could bear."

I cringed. "How can that happen? I thought you said the world would be plunged into chaos if Death left his position."

Michael took my hand and started to walk us back down the hall.

"Yes. That's true, but a replacement has already been selected."

I stumbled. "A replacement? For Death?"

"Yes."

I was speechless. And Michael, too, chose to say no more as we made our way out of the castle.

My thoughts were a chaotic mess as I tried to process how

this was even possible. I couldn't imagine how it would be to have a new person serving as Death. Would they look the same? Would they grow to despise the position just as their predecessor had? I shook my head, contemplating the fallout.

This is so not a good idea.

Michael came to a stop just outside the pearly gates.

My head snapped up, and I sucked in a breath.

Garrett and Holli strode in our direction, regal and fully dressed for their new positions. Death, in his suit and tie, and his Queen, in a beautiful red gown.

"Oh my God, Garrett! You're going to be Death?"

"Seems so," he lifted the scythe he now held and smiled wide. "Holli and I were sitting in Michael's home when suddenly, I was transported to the golden room. Death was there and relinquished the position and the magic that came with it. Apparently, it had to be offered freely before the transition would work. Once I negotiated my conditions, I accepted their offer and received my marks from Heaven and Hell."

"What conditions?" I asked.

"That Holli be allowed to serve at my side, retaining her memories as they are, and that I don't lose my life force the longer I serve." Garrett smiled. "After what's happened, they agreed that my happiness and the addition of Holli and Svell to our kingdom, will only help ensure its safety in case Loki tries

223

to return."

Garrett pulled Holli to him, gently placing his lips to hers.

My heart melted.

I was so happy he'd found someone to share his life with. I reached back for Michael's hand, sighing as it slid into mine. I turned to face him, ready to move on with my life as well. "I accept your offer on one condition."

His sexy smile weakened my knees. "What condition is that?"

"That we be able to visit Garrett and Holli all the time, whenever I want."

"That sounds reasonable." He pulled me to him and kissed me fiercely while spinning us into the air.

I looked back when I heard Garrett's voice, laced with his newfound power.

"Reasonable? Look at us, Raven." He smiled. "There's nothing reasonable about this entire situation. You're a Grim Reaper with the power to save people and are dating the leader of Heaven's army, and my girlfriend is the demon Goddess Hel who now resides in Purgatory with a frigid shadow-beast as her pet." He shook his head and started to laugh.

I joined in, cracking up at the oddness of our situation.

Reasonable? Maybe not...but perfectly right nonetheless.

The End

About the Author

Bestselling and Award-Winning Author, Tish Thawer, writes paranormal romances for all ages. From her first paranormal cartoon, Isis, to the Twilight phenomenon, myth, magic, and superpowers have always held a special place in her heart.

Tish is known for her detailed world-building and magic-laced stories. Her work has been compared to Nora Roberts, Sam Cheever, and Charlaine Harris. She has received nominations for a RONE Award (Reward of Novel Excellence), and Author of the Year (Fantasy, Dystopian, Mystery), as well as nominations and wins for Best Cover, and Reader's Choice Award.

Tish has worked as a computer consultant, photographer, and graphic designer, and is a columnist for Gliterary Girl media and has bylines in RT Magazine and Literary Lunes Magazine. She resides in Colorado with her husband and three wonderful children and is represented by Gandolfo, Helin, and Fountain Literary Management.

You can find out more about Tish and her all titles by visiting: www.TishThawer.com and subscribing to her newsletter at www.tishthawer.com/subscribe

Also by Tish Thawer

The Rose Trilogy
Scent of a White Rose – Book 1
Roses & Thorns – Book 1.5
Blood of a Red Rose – Book 2
Death of a Black Rose – Book 3

The Ovialell Series

Aradia Awakens - Book 1

Prophecy's Child - Companion

The Rise of Rae - Companion

Shay and the Box of Nye - Companion

Behind the Veil - Omnibus

The Women of Purgatory

Dark Abigail - Book 2

The Witches of BlackBrook

The Witches of BlackBrook - Book 1
The Daughters of Maine - Book 2

Collections

Christmas Lites II

Losing It: A Collection of V-Cards

Fairy Tale Confessions

Dance With Me

Turn the page for the opening scene from

QUEEN OF THE WITCHES

(Ovialell #2)

by

Tish Thawer

(Coming Soon)

QUEEN OF THE WITCHES

(Ovialell #2)

PROLOGUE

Devin watched as Aryiah held a glowing book above her head, and listened as the crowd began to cheer.

When she'd heard the Goddess announce that her precious Aradia had returned and eliminated the vampire assassin, it had taken every ounce of her will power to not fly out from behind the stone pillar and start ripping out throats until she was soaked in blood and holding Aryiah's heart in her hand.

The only thing that held her back was the humor she found in the fact that they all truly believed this was over. Little did they know that when Aryiah destroyed Gage with Aradia's magick, she inadvertently made Devin practically unstoppable.

The Darkling had been right. The bond she and Gage shared had indeed been special. They were connected through his dark magick and now...that magick was hers. When Aryiah had stood victorious, demanding her to leave, the shock she had felt wasn't from her previous friend's words, but from the surge of magick that had flowed into her at the moment of Gage's death.

So, let them have their party and celebrate, because soon enough...she would have her revenge.

(Psalm 19:1 NASB 1995)

God saw all that He had made, and behold, it was very good. And there was evening and there was morning, the sixth day.

(Genesis 1:31 NASB 1995)

For since the creation of the world His invisible attributes, His eternal power and divine nature, have been clearly seen, being understood through what has been made, so that they are without excuse.

(Romans 1:20 NASB 1995)

And when they heard this, they lifted their voices to God with one accord and said, "O Lord, it is You who MADE THE HEAVEN AND THE EARTH AND THE SEA, AND ALL THAT IS IN THEM,

(Acts 4:24 NASB 1995)

LOOK AROUND

There are so many big activities going on in our lives that we may forget to notice the little things around us. These small happenings or items can be hidden blessings that we only need to look for more closely. For example, are there flowers outside your door to enjoy? Do you have birds nesting in your trees that you can observe? Is there something about the weather you can enjoy? Pay attention to your environment and seek out what you can be thankful for now. Ask the Lord to help make you more aware of the blessings in your day. The more you look around, the more you will notice.

Dear Lord, keep my focus on You and Your creation. Lift my head to see the beauty of Your handiwork and to be reminded that You have good things for me today. Thank You for Your faithfulness in sharing Your blessings with me. Amen.

... The heavens are telling the glory of God;
And their expanse is declaring the work of his hands.

MEDICATION MIX-UPS

And there were shepherds living out in the fields nearby, keeping watch over their flocks at night.

(Luke 2:8 NIV)